D1180125

The Tamarack Tree

The

Tamarack Tree

Betty Underwood

Illustrated by Bea Holmes

1971

Houghton Mifflin Company Boston

To my mother —
who, by example and encouragement,
inspired me to write;

and

To my father —
whose stories of his boyhood gave me
my first feeling for history.

The Tamarack Tree

chapter 1

✟✟✟✟✟✟✟

The stagecoach rumbled into the inn's driveway, swallowed up by its own dust.

Coughing, Bernadette waved away the brown cloud which rushed into the window. She stuck her head out before the dust settled. Pittsfield, Massachusetts, and her long journey nearly done!

But where was the man who was to meet her? How could she possibly pick out the right stranger from the cluster of open-mouthed folks who waited at the hostelry door in this sleepy mountain village?

She was the last one out of the coach, since she'd had the window seat. The old lady in front of her groaned as she crawled down the high step to the ground. The girl knew the groan was from aching bones, because aching bones and jolting stagecoaches traveled together.

Bernadette stood uncertainly to one side, a big-eyed wisp of a fourteen-year-old girl in a stained purple wincey travel dress and a battered bonnet. Inside, she felt a churning that was half eagerness and a lot fear.

She tried not to stare at each unknown face, but for the life of her she couldn't keep from it. After all, she would live under the roof of one of these strangers, help his wife, perhaps even have the luck to feel part of his family. And most of all, go to school!

Was it that one? No, too young.

Or that one?

A lumbering, leather-faced man dressed in a short coat and low-crowned hat rather than the town-style high beaver, walked toward her, his shoes creaking protestingly. His square farmer's face with its peering blue eyes wore a cautious smile.

"Bernadette Savard?"

"Yes, sir."

"I'm Mr. David Fry. I knew it had to be you. My brother said you were a spirited cricket with brown hair and twinkly eyes. Where's your trunk?"

Shyly she pointed out her scuffed box to him, then slipped out of the crowd of passengers who elbowed one another at the stagecoach boot. In order not to stare impertinently at Mr. Fry, she watched the red-faced coachman tramp up and down to limber his legs stiffened from sitting too many hours on the high driver's seat.

Mr. Fry came back bent-over from carrying her little haircloth trunk. "Are you hungry?" he asked.

Now that they'd found each other, suddenly she realized she was ravenous. But she only nodded, lest she seem greedy.

They went into the inn's common room and sat down at a trestle table. Mr. Fry asked the tavern keeper for a plate of johnnycakes and a pitcher of scalding tea.

"Yes, you're just as my brother described you." David Fry rubbed his chin reflectively. "Said you were an earnest and good worker, strong for your size and spry. But warned us we weren't to let the dimples fool us — you had a mind of your own."

She ducked her head in embarrassment. "I guess I do," she confessed.

He stopped staring at her, his mind apparently decided. "Well, not too strong-headed to be lovable. Leastways, my brother wrote he was as fond of you as one of his own. My brother's family is thriving, then?"

"Oh, yes. All of them, sir. Ruth and Naomi help their ma in the kitchen and Jonathan looks after the stock and does haying now. The little ones are growing up fast."

"His church keeps my brother busy?"

"Yes, sir. It doesn't have as many members as Pastor would like, but after all, the Firelands are just beginning to fill up with people. The deep woods are coming down. Pastor Fry says it's a blessed relief to see those huge trees felled and the sunshine let into the fields."

"Hmmmm. Wish it were as easy to get rid of Connecticut rock," David Fry allowed. "Don't expect I'll ever see those Ohio forests. I missed my chance to go West when my brother did. Still, Connecticut's a good place and Canterbury the best spot in it."

"I expect so, sir."

Though he had an amiable air, Bernadette could tell David Fry wasn't a talkative man. Reserved, he was. Not like his brother, who was teasy, bear-huggy, affectionate. Better to leave this one now to his johnnycakes and tea.

Eating gave her time to think, too. Most girls in her place would be scared witless, but she'd been an orphan since she was three and long ago she'd grown used to the pain of it.

For years she'd been a hop and a skip ahead of an orphanage. First she'd lived in Montreal with a French cousin.

Then on her American side, Great Uncle Marcus Gray had brought her down to live with him and his wife on their frontier Ohio farm.

But Great Uncle and Aunt were elderly and a young child was bother for them, so Pastor Robb Fry — from the boundless latitude of an understanding heart — had offered to take her into the settlement to live with him and his family. Pastor had told Great Uncle Marcus it was a crime the farm was too far away for her to be schooled, said it was especially important for an orphan to be trained to do something — take in sewing, work a factory loom, have a dame school — for an orphan might have to make her way alone in the world. Fortunately, Uncle Marcus and Pastor Fry hadn't leaned toward needles or looms and the conclusion was that Pastor Fry would see if she had the wits for a schoolmarm. There was nothing more respectable for a lone female than teaching school, Pastor Fry had assured.

So she had moved into the settlement with the fun-loving Frys, fun-loving by nature even if they were supposed to be believers in original sin with damnation of infants. At the Frys' she had been treated like family, which was very lucky, for she knew orphans were generally valued just for the work they did. She soon grew to love saucy little Mrs. Fry, to love the mischievous Fry children as brothers and sisters.

She'd gone to the settlement school and caught up in a hurry. With a keen eye Pastor had watched how she learned. Then one night he'd gotten down one of his Yale books and begun to teach her Latin, and last year what he had remembered of his Greek. By candlelight they'd even had fine times working algebra problems; learning from Pastor was like playing games.

Bernadette sensed Pastor had enjoyed their lessons immensely but after a while she'd wondered why he didn't teach Latin to his own daughters. It dawned on her he might have offered but been turned down, when she overheard Ruth say to Naomi that Latin was for maiden ladies — no married female needed to know a word of Latin. Who had the most beaux in the settlement? Bernadette pondered. Ruth had.

Sitting in the Pittsfield Inn, Bernadette swallowed hard. It had been terrible saying good-bye to Pastor Fry. Pastor had patted her on the back and reminded her she was going not only to live and work with his brother in a more civilized place, but — at Uncle Marcus's expense — would attend a fine female seminary as well. When she'd stood on tiptoe to kiss Pastor Fry, she'd loved him more than anyone in the world. He was the closest to home she'd ever known.

What a trip she'd had! How exciting the Erie Canal had been, with its locks and tow horses and snub-nosed racing packets! Albany had been huge. She would never have found the Pittsfield stage if a friend of Pastor's hadn't hurried her through the bustling streets, with their shouting canal hawkers and loaded farm carts.

Well, someday she'd go back to Ohio and its Firelands. After all, that's where her dreams lay.

Meantime, it was better to pretend the tears in her eyes came from the hot tea and not the remembering.

When they heard the new coachman's shout, she and Mr. Fry rushed outside. This coachman was also red faced and choleric. He wiped his mouth, then climbed self-importantly to his seat and sat haughtily, fingering a new whiplash. A fresh matched pair stood harnessed to the coach. Bernadette's

little trunk was hurriedly transferred to the boot and she and David Fry crowded up to the coach door. New straw lay on the floor of the cumbersome wooden box swaying from its frayed strap hinges. People were settling themselves on the hard seats. Some were already striking up conversation. The two of them had hardly squeezed in when Bernadette felt weight thrown on the tall hind wheels. With a mighty grumble, the reluctant wheels began to turn.

She and David Fry talked at first. Right off, she asked him about the Canterbury female seminary. David Fry said he'd let his wife, Hester, tell her all about *that*. But he'd just as soon she wouldn't ask Hester about school till after the baby came.

"Is Mrs. Fry against my going?" Bernadette wondered in sudden apprehension.

"Of course not," David assured her. "But 'tis more comforting for Hester to think of you home with her and the baby, not off at school all day. God willing, we do want this child," he finished humbly.

She settled back, relieved. She could understand how that could be. They talked of different things.

In the blue shadows of the June countryside, they crossed from Massachusetts into Connecticut, traversed the immense city of Hartford, coached through Willimantic and Scotland, and came at last to the village of Canterbury.

She didn't pay much attention to Canterbury except to notice it was a dignified armada of great houses anchored around a crossroads. She didn't notice because she was too busy secretly studying David Fry's son, Paul, who had come to the village to fetch them home in the farm wagon.

Paul was a tall stripling with freckles, bright blue eyes,

and a sandy thatch of hair. He sat sober as a judge on the high wagon seat when she and his father climbed up beside him. The cat had made off with his tongue so it now made off with hers. But she knew something special which might account for Paul's being unsociable. For fifteen years he'd been brought up alone. Between him and the baby his mother, Hester, now carried in her, there were no children except four dead ones. In Ohio, Pastor had looked ever so sober speaking to Bernadette of it.

The wagon braked down the Plainfield Road to the Quinebaug River where they stopped to pay their toll. Then, with Paul slapping the rump of the horse, they climbed up what Mr. Fry said was Black Hill, turned at the top of the ridge, and jounced over a country trail to the farm.

The farm sat facing a vast rolling meadow which fell to the south. The faded yellow house was flat faced, square, and dignified. There were weathered outbuildings and a gray barn which wasn't hooked to the house the way so many barns in these parts were. On one side was an apple orchard. On the other, a lovely grove of pine trees. Trees back here were puny whips compared to the enormous virgin hardwoods of Ohio, but the New England evergreens fascinated Bernadette — soft as velvet far away, they were full of prickly needles close up.

At the kitchen door, a chunky black-haired woman appeared. Used as she thought she was to new roofs and families, Bernadette still experienced a strangled sensation of fear.

"Welcome, Bernadette." The woman held out her arms in a motherly, sweet gesture that went with her plump, matronly face. Bernadette felt a great load lift from her as

Hester Fry held her off and looked at her with friendly gray eyes full of unspoken sympathy.

Upstairs in her own little eaved room with its rag rug, tall chest, and narrow bed, she unpacked her small trunk. Despite Hester's warmth, heartsickness engulfed her and she longed to be back in Ohio with Pastor Fry's family. Then she reminded herself she'd see them again, all of them. Her woolly mood cleared as she hurried downstairs to help fix supper.

Hester Fry chatted cheerfully while she showed Bernadette the kitchen, pump and butter room, and pantry. She kept up her easy talk all through supper, explaining how the farm had been in the Fry family for three generations, mentioning neighbors, saying casual things about the church or the general store in Canterbury. Bernadette's quick curiosity — how Pastor Fry had teased her about her inquisitiveness! — stirred. Perhaps Hester Fry herself would mention Miss Prudence Crandall's seminary for young ladies. But Hester didn't remark on school.

She turned hopeful dark eyes on Paul. Maybe Paul would think to speak of school. But Paul didn't speak of anything. Though he was a hearty eater, he continued to be silence itself. As soon as he could, he bolted out to finish an evening chore. Watching Paul disappear, Bernadette longed for Jonathan Fry in Ohio. Jonathan was also fifteen but had been like a brother to her, a fond, teasing brother. She could ask Jonathan anything. And usually did, he sometimes grumbled, half laughing.

Well, it was too early to tell about Paul Fry, Bernadette reminded herself sensibly.

She and Hester and David Fry sat out on the kitchen

stoop till David yawned. Everyone knew what it meant when the master of the house yawned.

From her bedroom window she watched a big yellow moon glow behind wagging leaves. Since she wasn't sleepy, Bernadette sat down on the floor and put her chin in her fist on the windowsill. She felt alone and empty. To fill herself up, she recalled why she was here.

To help, yes. That was always expected of an orphan.

But to go to school: that was the fire shut up in her bones!

She wasn't just going to the seminary in Canterbury either. After Canterbury she was determined to return to Ohio.

What would she do back there?

Go to college. Just thinking of it still took her breath away. In 1833, all over the world no girls went to college. Yet she, Bernadette Savard, meant to go to college. Go to the institute in the forest.

Oberlin, it was called.

She never stirred a muscle while the low yellow moon sailed higher, changing to silver. She was remembering.

Bernadette waited for the settlement teacher, old Jimmy O'Connor, to wake up. After lunch he always dozed. Once Jonathan Fry and the big boys had dropped flies in Jimmy's open mouth while he snored. But when Jimmy O'Connor had waked up, Jonathan and the others had had to crawl four times around the stove on hands and knees, and each time they went by the teacher they got a blistering from a stick of wood. After that Jonathan found an old piece of buckskin to line his pantaloons. Helped with the splinters on the school benches, too, he'd told Bernadette; then he'd asked Bernadette what she did about splinters. Bernadette hadn't been shocked; she'd just said after the first two or three times she'd learned to sit down easy.

I wish he'd wake up, Bernadette worried. The big boys were getting restless.

"Jonathan Fry!" the teacher roared, rearing up like he'd been shot out of a cannon. "Recite the Latin cases!"

Oh, dear! Jonathan wouldn't know them, Bernadette realized. Pastor had tried and tried with Jonathan . . .

Nominative, genative, dative, she murmured anxiously to herself.

Mr. O'Connor wouldn't let Jonathan sit down till he'd humiliated him with the accusative and ablative, too. Jonathan Fry, who was so-so in Mr. Webster's blue-back spelling book and Mr. Morse's *Geography Made Easy,* was only a whiz when it came to ciphering out of *Pike's Arithmetic.* Still, even if Jonathan excelled at ciphering, it bothered Pastor to be sending a son back to Yale who was a dunce in Latin.

Bernadette knew Jimmy O'Connor wouldn't call on her to recite the Latin cases. The teacher bragged he was one itinerant schoolmaster who knew his Latin, but she knew her own Latin was beginning to make Schoolmaster O'Connor nervous.

Marthie Purdy nudged Bernadette and Mr. O'Connor caught Marthie at it.

"Marthie Purdy, you march over there!" Mr. O'Connor pointed sternly. Marthie knew what to do; she found the bored auger hole nearest her nose height and gingerly fit her face to the hole. She had to bend her knees to stand there. Bernadette felt sorry for Marthie — she'd only had that punishment once and knew it was dreadfully tiresome.

11

Fervently, Bernadette wished school were done for the day. Spring was leaving hints on ground and trees, and the sheep were pawing old drifts to get at the green beneath.

It was time to copy in her copybook. She struggled with a goose-quill pen and watery maple-bark ink. Mr. O'Connor asked Hannah Sowers to bound Africa, and once more Hannah got the Capes of Good Hope and Horn mixed up. Poor Hannah, she tried so hard — maybe because her family scoffed at girls going to school, and didn't let her come very often. Baxter Graham forgot what an adverb was. For Friday's exercises, Bernadette was assigned the same old declamation — Mrs. Hemans's "Landing of the Pilgrim Fathers."

The schoolmaster limped to the stove and cracked it with the poker. It was the sign Bernadette had longed for; three o'clock and school was out! She rushed for the door, snatched her cloak from the peg, and was released to the sweet smell of fresh, bright air.

She was bounding out of the school yard to catch up with Jonathan when a tall man on horseback cantered toward her. Where was Pastor Fry going in such a hurry?

"Bernadette, come along! I want to take you to Oberlin with me."

To Oberlin? Her mouth fell open in surprise. That was the new collegiate institute they were trying to hack out of the forest of Russia township a few miles away. Why should Pastor Fry want to take her to that place? Everyone was saying terrible things about it.

He pulled her up on the pillion behind his saddle and slapped the horse, which bolted so fast she had to grab Pastor's coat to keep from falling off.

"We have to hurry," he warned. "I don't want to be caught on that trail late at night. But I want to go there before the mud gets worse."

She didn't blame him about the mud. In another month, with spring rains, a horse would be up to his knees in the potholes.

Their speed and the state of the clay-covered, split-rail road kept her from asking why they were going to Oberlin. Anyway, sometimes it didn't pay to ask Pastor Fry too many questions. When he had his mind on *things,* then it was best to respect his preoccupations. So she bounced along on the pillion feeling like a gourd seed.

Soon the woods began to close darkly around them, a solid wall of growth rearing out of a swampy plain. In the school yard there'd been a spun-gold sunlight, delicate and luminous. Now they entered a cavelike world of moss-green shade.

"Bernadette, I meant to bring you here sooner, but I had to go out to the farm and talk to your Uncle Marcus Gray first," Pastor finally spoke over his shoulder to her. "Your uncle agrees with me, says he'll pay so you can attend Oberlin after you've had the rest of your schooling."

Attend Oberlin?

It was the most astounding thing anyone had ever suggested to her.

Instantly, she tried to recall all the things she'd heard about Oberlin. There were plenty to recall!

It was to be a college where impoverished boys of good mind and character could get a Christian education — its motto was to be "Learning and Labor." That part didn't bother a soul, but all the passionate local arguing came because it was going to let in poor *girls* of good mind and character, too. Oberlin declared it would be the first college in the world to elevate the female character.

It was a monstrous scandal, Schoolmaster O'Connor declared. Some settlement folk fell in with the schoolmaster, even vowed they would raid the colony and pull down the college buildings as soon as they were built. Cleveland's leading newspaper said the project was immoral.

But just a fortnight ago — after a protracted period of absent-mindedness — Pastor Fry had climbed into his pulpit and put himself in blunt opposition to Oberlin's enemies. Pastor Fry had argued that Christian women should be taught properly. The point he had made, which Bernadette now remembered most vividly, was that out here on the frontier it was hard to come by respectable men schoolteachers; dedicated women were needed in the log schoolhouses of Ohio. Then he'd ended his sermon on a canny note. Women teachers could be hired for half a man's keep. Everyone knew that the Firelands folk were strapped for money.

When the trail to Oberlin narrowed into a track of cleared underbrush crisscrossed by huge roots, Pastor Fry tied the horse and they walked through the forest the last quarter of a mile.

They came at last to a large clearing. In the late-afternoon light it was a shambles of giant felled trees, trunks lying every which way, fires smouldering. A pair of newly raised cabins clung together in the smoky twilight. Before he rapped on one of the doors, Pastor Fry pointed out to Bernadette where the first college building would rise and how

14

several more were to fit in. He said the village would ring the campus square, Oberlin being founded as a Christian community as well as a school.

She remembered how she'd stood there and tried to capture the picture in her head. But with such a shambles it was hard.

"It doesn't look very promising," he admitted. "But it will soon. The trustees expect Oberlin Hall to be finished by fall. Then the doors can open for the first students."

Suddenly he stooped beside her and she was startled by the tender, yearning look his face wore. She realized now how much he wished Jonathan — yes, and Ruth and Naomi — cared about learning.

"At first," he went on, "I thought of your getting just enough education for country-school teaching. But then I found you had a mind for better. Country-school teaching is hard and lonely and ill rewarded. The more I pondered, the more this Oberlin institute seemed the answer for you. At Oberlin you could learn enough to establish a fine female academy, Bernadette, perhaps in a proper New England town away from rude dangers."

Then he'd told her about Canterbury and how she could prepare for college there while attending a fine female seminary. She would live with his brother's family and be special help to them at their time of anxiety.

Rooted to the spot, Bernadette felt she couldn't bear another parting.

Ever understanding, Pastor put his arm around her shoulder and rubbed his scratchy whiskers against her cheek. "Little one, we shan't let you slip away from us."

15

After that, she could think of what he proposed, think of the doors he was opening to her. What he said, once implanted in her, began to bloom beauteously.

Finally it had become as much a driving part of her as her flesh, her blood, her bone.

She'd be a schoolmarm, have a school of her own, teach other girls the things she took fierce delight in learning. Other girls who must feel like she did, that there wasn't a place in the world for them. Despite Ruth and Naomi Fry, something deep in Bernadette told her there must be legions of girls who felt dissatisfied and dispossessed; she believed they were everywhere.

She and Pastor Fry had supper with one of the families in the cabins. There were older girls in that family and they were going to Oberlin. One of the girls said three females were planning to walk eight miles every day from Elyria to Oberlin if they had to . . .

By the light of a strip of shellbark lit from the hearth, the brave family in the clearing bade them good-bye, their faces at the door dyed by the ruddy firelight. Using his little pierced lantern, she and Pastor Fry walked down the forest trail to his tethered horse.

She held the lantern with one hand and hung to his coat with the other. A bobcat screamed suddenly from a nearby tree and she nearly jumped out of her skin. But there was no sign of fear from the man she clung to. Nothing in the world seemed to frighten Pastor Fry.

Bernadette wouldn't be frightened either. It was the least return she could make to one who had given her a sense of herself. More than that — had given her a great goal to make up for being alone.

16

An owl hooted softly. Time to stop her remembering. The moon in Canterbury hung high.

chapter 2

✤✤✤✤✤✤✤

THE CHAISE JOUNCED through highland pastures. The fields were different from the ones in Ohio, Bernadette observed. Instead of flat and square, they were odd shaped and climbed around curves to disappear behind blue hills. If there was outcropping, it was rock, not a blackened tree stump. And Connecticut fences were serpentine lines of gray stones, not marching split rails.

By the roadside, June bloomed in a profusion of daisies, Queen Anne's lace, and blue cornflowers. Golden fiddle-heads were beginning to bud even though August was a long way off. Eagerly Bernadette sniffed the world; it smelled new and succulent, not yet scorched by July's heat or seared by August's high noons. Far below, the Quine-baug River flashed in the sun.

She sat stiff as a poker between David and Paul Fry. Soberly, silently, they were going to church. She recollected when the Ohio Frys went to church everyone was limber and jolly. Sometimes Bernadette was the jolliest of all as she good-humoredly twitched little Fry bonnets and caps, giggled with Naomi, or covertly banged Jonathan with her Bible when his teasing got sassy.

Bernadette missed Hester's comfortable company. But

Hester had stayed behind since buggy riding was dangerous for her and the unborn baby. Not many more days for Hester to wait. Fervently Bernadette hoped this time the child would live.

Hoped it so much she'd firmly checkreined her torrent of school questions. And hadn't Hester herself volunteered a remark to Bernadette? "I've promised David I wouldn't fret about your school before the baby comes. We'll talk of it afterward." Afterward. After the baby. The baby meant so much to Hester; it was there in her troubled gray eyes.

They turned off the country lane onto the pebbled pike. Bernadette couldn't wait to get to town. She felt now as if she'd never had a real look at it.

David spanked the horse into a lively trot when they got to Main Street. Bernadette clasped her French Bible and studied the tree-dappled road they wheeled down. Canterbury was awesomely elegant, its commodious houses set to the backs of sweeping lawns. Up on the slope ahead stood a handsome white-spired church.

"Which one's Miss Crandall's school?" The question exploded out of her.

Paul nodded in the direction of a beautiful house with a white fence and gates, fanlit-shuttered door, rounded window above its entry, high, square-built roof with imposing double chimneys. Why, it had a fountain! Bernadette craned her neck to look back in disbelief.

"It's the biggest house in the village," she breathed.

"That's a fact," David Fry agreed between compressed lips. Was there a strange quality in David Fry's voice? A note of bitterness?

But why in the world bitterness?

They rolled up the church drive. David stopped to let her and Paul hop down at the front steps. He drove around to the carriage sheds.

"Paul, what's the girls' school like?"

"Like? It's a deal of a mess right now. What do you want to go to school for anyway? I hate school."

"I want to go more than anything," she answered simply.

"How come?"

"Because I want to have a girls' school, a seminary of my own. Your Uncle Robb thinks girls should have a chance at learning. I do, too. Besides, I'm going to college."

"Going to college!" he nearly yelled in dismay. "I never heard of such a thing!"

"I know," she answered with a patience beginning to be born of necessity. "But what about Miss Crandall's school? Why do you say it's a deal of a mess?"

"Well, it is," was all Paul replied. "Here comes Pa. We're nearly the last ones in. They'll close the doors on us."

They wouldn't be quite the last ones in, she saw. Hurrying up the church slope was a decorous procession — three men in black frock coats, high-necked cravats, tall, brushed-beaver hats. Men escorting wives in puff-sleeved, ankle-length dresses, each of which rustled over its half-dozen starched petticoats. Following the grownups were a covey of young boys in tight bobtailed jackets. Behind the boys were three swaddled girls in pantalettes. The young ones minced from the imprisonment of their feet in Sunday's shoes.

When they entered the church vestibule, Bernadette's first

thought was that Pastor Fry just ought to see this Canterbury church. Then she was kind of glad he couldn't; things were hard enough out in Ohio.

Double doors off the foyer opened into the huge meeting room. There were not one, but two pulpits. The ceiling seemed very high; the white-painted pews far beneath were a regular maze. A balcony ran around three sides; she guessed a thousand could be seated up and down. Six sets of paned windows were on each wall. At Pastor's rude settlement meetinghouse, light could scarcely penetrate the narrow openings. On a dark winter's day, they had to burn candles — tallow dips screwed down on old fork tines nailed to the whitewashed log walls.

Once in the Fry pew, Bernadette studied the Canterbury people. A lot fancier than settlement folk, that was for sure. She had just got her unruly roving glance under control when her mind was abruptly jerked from guilty piety back to the lively world again.

The great bell above was tolling its warning that the doors would stand unbolted only a minute more, when footsteps sounded at the back of the church. Soft footsteps marching in cadence down the aisle.

Bernadette glanced over her shoulder, gave a little gasp, hastily smothered her indrawn breath. Her head swiveled to follow the progress of a group of girls who moved into a row of pews directly across from where she sat.

Black girls!

Around her bonnet brim she surreptitiously counted them: twelve, thirteen, fourteen . . . Fourteen Negro girls! Their dark skins looked wildly alien in this bleach-faced place.

For that matter, they looked alien even to their own prim outfits of softly colored muslin.

But whoever they were, they weren't strangers to the stiff propriety of the time. As soon as each girl sat down she folded her hands and grew motionless.

A white woman had followed them. As this woman settled herself, she appeared unaware of the shock she and the Negroes had caused; she, too, was soon a picture of un-moving attentiveness.

Bernadette felt waves of emotion rush through the church, waves which finally ebbed in an undertow of hushed whisper-ing, restless creaking of pew backs, uncomfortable nose blow-ing.

She just *had* to take a final peek, moving her eyes only far enough so as not to crane her neck. She guessed the Negroes ranged in age from ten to eighteen. Only their profiles were clear, but these were fascinating in their dark variety: the purple-black snub-nose of one contrasted with the high-yellow, aquiline outline of another. Most were round and chestnut brown, Bernadette concluded.

Trailing his black frock, the minister suddenly climbed into the high pulpit. He stood there and fixed his congrega-tion with a steely eye. All stirring promptly ceased.

The minister opened an enormous Bible for the scripture reading. When his voice began, its thin harshness surprised Bernadette. A pang of homesickness for Pastor Fry's deep, warm, vibrant tones shot through her.

The reading was the puzzling Genesis story of Noah. Noah, who had cursed into eternal servitude his grandson — Ham's son, Canaan — because Noah had been seen drunk and uncovered by Ham.

Innocently Bernadette tried to probe the Holy Word. It was most shameful and disgusting to be drunk and uncovered; it would be misery for a son to see his father thus. But was not the fault Noah's in the first place for getting drunk? Why should punishment come not to Noah, but to Ham — and not even to Ham, but to Canaan, the helpless son of Ham?

How would the pastor's sermon explain the words of Genesis? But when the sermon commenced, Bernadette realized in disappointment the minister wasn't going to explain who was really guilty of what. What the Canterbury pastor did instead was dwell endlessly on punishment — he positively relished describing God's ways of chastising. She was glad Pastor Fry preached differently, it kept her from fidgeting fearfully as Paul was doing.

"Who was Canaan?" finally shrilled this new pastor. "He was Ham's descendant, cursed of God and his skin dyed black. His shoulder was set to the yoke of service. The African is Canaan's descendant, the African who offended the Almighty through Noah. Slavery is his curse; he cannot escape God's curse. The Holy Word tells us this. Who among us dares to deny the judgment of God?"

At last Bernadette caught the drift of the Bible lesson! Why, it was aimed right at the dark girls who sat across the aisle! The minister was telling them they were meant to be bought and sold because in ages past an old, drunken man had cursed them.

Bernadette shifted uneasily. The sermon seemed a cruel thing to address to those who were caught and helpless. When she peeked she saw the black girls weren't merely quiet now, they were stone carved. Only the white woman with them betrayed emotion. As Bernadette watched, a frown flickered across her face. Who was she? And where had so many black girls come from in a village like Canterbury? Full of thought, Bernadette forgot to sing.

What did she know about Negroes? she asked herself. She tried to remember when she had seen her first one, but couldn't. There had been a handful of Negroes in Montreal — American ones — escaped from the Southland. There were a few escaped slaves in the Firelands, ones who'd stopped off before they got to Lake Erie. She'd rarely seen them.

She peeked again. She thought the girls' dark faces odd. No, not odd, her honest mind admitted, but coarse and unrefined. How could you tell if they were clean? Whether a person was clean or dirty was one quick way you could measure what sort the person was.

But cleanliness wasn't all that mystified her. There was something very complex about black things. Dark, mysterious places like old cellars, closets smelling strangely, woods too thick for light, nighttime, when dreadful shapes lurked outside the house . . .

Were black things wicked and immoral then? Weren't the angels of our Lord always clothed in shining white? And the forces of evil arrayed in sable black? By now she was staring at the girls as though to find an answer in them.

Unexpectedly, one of the older blacks turned. Their glances collided. The dark girl looked away, disdain in her glance for the other's rude curiosity.

After that, Bernadette paid a shamed attention to the end of the service. Even tried to lose herself in the long, long final prayer . . .

24

Afternoon came: she rose with David and Paul. But she saw that no one was moving into the aisles except the Negro girls, who, after waiting in confusion a moment, filed slowly from their pews. The congregation stood in a body and watched them go. Again Bernadette sensed a great wall of unspoken hostility.

Most of the dark eyes were cast down meekly. But Bernadette saw the one she had stared at step forth, head high. The white woman, her jaw set and her face flushed from the hard looks of the church folk, led the girls to the door.

With the last girl gone, indignant voices burst from all sides like water rushing from a dammed-up reservoir.

"Whose were they?" Bernadette turned to Paul.

Paul's face looked like a thunderclap. "The schoolmarm's," he snapped. "What did you think?"

"Schoolmarm's?" she asked, confused. "What schoolmarm?"

"Come along, Bernadette," David Fry interrupted. "Let's go home."

While David went to get the chaise, Bernadette and Paul watched the black girls walk two by two down the church slope.

Suddenly the calm was shattered by a startling staccato sound. A drum rolled with a stridence. From behind one of the big houses across the road Bernadette spied a young drummer and several half-grown boys. One of them brandished a long-handled musket.

Instinct told her who their target was.

Horrified, she looked back to the little group of black girls. Oh, surely they would pick up their skirts and flee drum and musket as fast as they could!

25

But the black girls and the white woman moved slowly across the green, never breaking step. The drum kept up its mocking march.

Maddened by such unconcern the musket was fired. The boys chanted raucously, "Go home! Go home!"

Hardly breathing, Bernadette waited for worse to happen. She prayed that it would not.

The girls were headed for the beautiful schoolhouse with its leaping silver fountain. Headed for Miss Crandall's fine seminary where she, Bernadette Savard, was going to school.

She tugged frantically at Paul Fry's sleeve, but he seemed mesmerized by the drummer and the black girls. Her pleading, "Do they belong there?" went unheeded by him.

The first black girls reached the big front door. It swung open; they disappeared into the shadowed interior of the house. Finally the last one passed from view.

There was one more mean drum tattoo before the little band of tormentors dashed off up the road.

Bernadette stumbled down the steps to David and the waiting chaise. But before she climbed in, she turned to look wonderingly at the folks from the church, many of whom were grouped outside, watching intently.

She never forgot the mass of faces, ferocious, sneering, pleased to witness such humiliation. Quickly, she glanced at Paul to see if he looked bothered. But he smirked the most.

David sat, tight lipped, holding the reins.

"Mr. Fry," she said, summoning all her courage, "I just *have* to know what's going on at the school."

"Get in," he urged. "I'll explain when we get home, when I've got my thoughts more composed."

Their ride was a silent, swift one.

chapter 3

🌲🌲🌲🌲🌲🌲🌲

I T WAS A GOOD MANY DAYS before David Fry explained to Bernadette. When they got home, the midwife motioned to them from the back stoop. Would Mr. Fry turn the chaise around and fetch the doctor at Canterbury — Mrs. Fry had begun.

"Paul, stay with me," David ordered. "Bernadette, you best get out in case you're needed here for water boiling or vittle cooking. We'll be back as soon as we can, but I fear I must chase down the doctor. He wasn't in his pew at church."

The midwife clomped up the stairs; Bernadette stood in the kitchen uncertainly. Then she got out the platters of Sunday cold things and after that she picked up the sock she was knitting. All the time she wondered what was happening upstairs.

Wondering, hoping . . .

Footsteps came clomping back down. The midwife put her head in the door and said, urgently, "Come with me, missy. I may need help before they get back."

Bernadette threw down her knitting, followed the midwife timidly.

Hester didn't rouse when they entered the bedroom; she seemed asleep. The cradle was made up with snow-white sheets and sat empty beside the four-poster bed.

The midwife seated herself in the rocking chair and instantly dozed. Bernadette crouched by the window and looked down the meadow. Connecticut was almost as hot as Ohio. She sighed nervously. How could Cousin Hester stand to lie in bed under those quilts?

Just as she asked herself the question, Hester heaved off the covers. Her rumpled bedgown was tangled all about her; she pushed at it impatiently. Under her gown a great mound showed. Bernadette didn't mean to stare.

The midwife opened an eye. "Here, now," she crooned, as though she were talking to a bad child. "You stop that."

The rocking chair squeaked; the old woman thumped over to the bed. Firmly she pulled the clothing straight around her patient. Hester groaned and wakened.

"Where's David?" she whispered.

"Coming," the midwife soothed. "Sleep again if you can."

"Bernadette, did I hear you come in?"

"Yes, Mrs. Fry."

"Pray, go outside, child."

"She'll stay a bit," the midwife explained matter-of-factly. "Till your man comes with the doctor I might have need of her."

Then like lightning, something came over Hester and she was no longer concerned who was in the room.

"Un . . . unh . . . unh," she suddenly moaned deep in her throat, the sound coming from between her clenched teeth. Bernadette saw it was pain that had stretched her tight.

Oh, Hester, don't do that, implored Bernadette. Where were the doctor and David? Bernadette felt she must flee this room, with its unknown terror . . .

29

"You help me," the old midwife ordered. "Something's happening at last. We don't want she should ruin the sheets."

The midwife brought old quilts and a yellow sheet. Together they got the sheet under Hester, who lifted herself as best she could while they rolled and spread. Hester kept her hands carefully over her body, her bedgown in its place.

Then the midwife brought a length of rope to the bed. Bernadette looked in confusion from rope to patient. What was it for? she wondered.

The midwife passed the rope through the foot slat and brought it up the length of the bed. She twisted it into a powerful knot and flopped it down on the quilt by Hester's side.

"There," she muttered, looking clinically down into Hester's closed-eyed face. "Now grab, Mrs. Fry . . ."

"Could I set the food in the pantry away from the flies?" Bernadette whispered.

"No, ma'am," the midwife answered bluntly. "I just can't spare you, child. This birth won't be an easy one; it could take the both of us to hold and help."

Bernadette soon saw what the rope was for. Hester hung onto it when it hurt the most . . . it began to hurt her worse now.

"Come nigh, girl. Bathe her face with this rag. It's blistering hot for birthing."

Hester sank back on the pillow. Her eyes, which just a second before seemed to see nothing, fought their way to the girl's face and focused there.

"I hope she's pretty like you," she murmured.

"We'll be lucky it be alive and kept alive, no matter how

30

it looks," the midwife muttered. "These Fry babies are born still. I've been here three times before."

While Bernadette was trying to fathom why Hester and David's babies were born motionless, there was commotion.

"It's broke," the midwife exclaimed in triumph, hands busy under the quilt.

Hester seized the rope and pulled hard on it. Bernadette saw she was commencing to work far harder than a man worked, even cradling wheat. Hester's face was heated, determined; she gritted her teeth.

One of the hard-work sounds ended on a low wail. Bernadette jumped, dropped the cloth, and started for the door.

The midwife didn't notice; she was busy fussing below. But before Bernadette had reached the door, she steeled herself and went back to her place at the head of the bed. Her duty to help was plain . . .

After that, time moved with the slowness of grains of sand building up in an hourglass bottom. It moved in Hester's spates of action, then her exhausted moments of collapse on the hot sheet.

The more tugging, the more pleased the midwife grew. Bernadette watched the dispassionate woman press and knead Hester's mountainous middle, pushing, prodding, her hands spread wide. But what she did couldn't seem to expel from its tight cage the being within. Bernadette concentrated on wringing out the cloth which comforted the flushed and labored face.

Where was David Fry? *Come,* she prayed.

Midafternoon . . .

More water was needed. Bernadette ran to the kitchen, ran back, sloshing water on the pine-board back steps.

31

As she came in the room, she couldn't help but see where the child would come from. While she stood, paralyzed, the dark crowned head first showed.

"Hold her!" the midwife yelled. Bernadette dropped the copper kettle on the floor and stumbled over it to the head of the bed. Involuntarily, she seized Hester's shoulders, felt the trembling of Hester's body in its mighty effort to release her child.

"Ah, good, good . . ." the midwife breathed, and below, between the raised legs, Bernadette couldn't take her eyes from the small, dark head.

After the head there was a curled-up, glistening, round body, and then the midwife was holding it by the feet and head. It was a slippery baby. The midwife slapped it; it opened its mouth and shrilled.

"Would the doctor was found," the midwife panted.

Suddenly there was a pounding on the stairs and the door burst open. David Fry stood there, breathing hard, seeing what was on the bed — his unconscious wife, the rumple she lay in, the body of his child . . .

"It's come." He groaned. "The doctor's following as soon as he can."

"Too late," the midwife answered. "Go outside. I'll call you when she's cleaned."

David whispered one thing: "Alive?"

"Both of them," the midwife snapped.

The midwife saw the overturned kettle on the floor.

"Water!" she commanded. Once again Bernadette dashed to the kitchen.

When she got back, the babe was cut loose from its coils; the midwife was sponging it, then she was putting a napkin around its tiny body and its thin arms into the little gown. It was alive; it was the girl child Hester had wanted.

"Here," the midwife said. The child was placed in Bernadette's arms. She felt the softness of it; she felt the power of it. It mewed like a kitten. And a piercing sense of miracle briefly blunted her new-found knowledge of the pain of how life began.

The midwife brought a fresh bedgown for Hester and got her feeble body with its empty husk into it. The soiled sheet was pulled from beneath her; gingerly, she was moved to the head of the bed. The quilt was pulled decently over her and her hair tucked under her cap. She lay with a face as still as death.

The baby wriggled; Bernadette watched its mother. Hester's eyes fluttered. They were human eyes again.

No one told her to do it, but she knew to do it anyway. Bernadette went up and laid the child down beside Hester. Hester turned to it as an animal nuzzles, smells, and licks its young. There were just the two of them, alone in a marvelous world.

"Alive?" the mother asked.

"Alive," the midwife declared. "And hearty, too."

"Girl?"

"Girl."

"Thank God," the faint voice whispered.

"David?"

"He's here, waiting to come in . . ."

David entered; Bernadette was forgotten. Quietly she crept down the stairs, seeing the slosh marks on the steps and remembering how they got there.

She went out to the farmyard and up the hill to the

orchard. It was midafternoon; bees — so many of them back here — hummed in the air.

She stopped walking because suddenly things spun around and the earth tilted crazily under the too-brilliant sky.

She realized it was only another step till she could stand under the first tree. Its cool limbs reached out to cover her; the sky, so vast and dazzling, was gone. The ground from which the trunk took root was level and solid as it had always been.

She leaned her head on the low branch, clinging to it.

She closed her eyes and fleetingly the thought came to her that the life of a woman must be split into two worlds: a secret world, a mysterious and inexorable world of storm; and this other calm world of earth and tree, richly known and visible.

Was there a meeting place for the two worlds? Bernadette needed to find this place.

She looked up and saw a chaise rushing up the lane, a cloud of dust blowing behind it.

It was the doctor, coming at last to deliver Hester Fry.

chapter 4

✝✝✝✝✝✝✝

THE SUN FLOWED into the empty sky drinking up the mist
which lay on the fields.

Bernadette turned from the dawn horizon and looked
around her room. Could she have been in this house only
two weeks? It seemed like two months.

She stole downstairs quietly. She passed the parlor in its
silent order, chairs and settees pushed straight against the
brown-paper walls; the high standup desk, which nobody
used, proudly open for inspection. Cracks of light from the
curtains — closed to prevent the rug from fading — sliced
across the Brussels carpet.

Soon Paul and David would come into the kitchen for
breakfast. Embers from last night should still be left in the
fireplace. As she knelt on the brick hearth she remembered
with longing Mrs. Fry's shining black cookstove out in Ohio.
Cookstoves were new, but Pastor liked mechanics and tinker-
ing and, over Mrs. Fry's objection, he'd ordered a stove
carted from Cleveland. The first time it was used, his women
could see how many hearth blisters they'd save. Still, there
was one thing this old-time kitchen boasted which Pastor's
had not. That was a well room with an inside pump. Bernadette carried the teakettle to the fire, thankful not to have to
lug heavy pails of water pumped from an outdoor well
sweep.

Upstairs the baby cried hungrily. There was stirring from Hester's and David's bedroom. Summertime kept a farmer busy ind David wouldn't linger to talk with his bedfast wife. Bernadette stirred the mush in the kettle, lifted it up a notch on the lug.

Paul came into the kitchen, closed-faced as usual. Bernadette had given up trying to figure whether he was scared of her or just felt superior to mere girls. Certainly Paul had resisted all her shy efforts to jolly with him or be his friend.

Now he said, "Ma wants you to take the pot off the crane and come upstairs."

Had she done something wrong? Bernadette wiped her hands hastily on her apron.

She knocked at the part-open door.

"Come," Hester called. Hester was sitting up against the pillows nursing the baby, Rachel. Flannel covered the mother's breast; all Bernadette could see was the silky top of baby Rachel's head. Such an alive small being, Rachel, sucking so lustily.

What else had Bernadette seen in this room? It was a blessing she forgot easily.

David Fry wore work clothes and a businesslike air.

"Bernadette," he began without preamble, "I've just had a chance to tell Hester what happened last Sabbath."

"David says the schoolmarm brought the Negro girls to church," Hester observed. "Said the Pastor addressed his sermon to the blacks and afterward village rapscallions drummed them to the school door and even fired a musket. David said the church folk watched it gladly."

"Yes, ma'am. It happened that way."

Drummed the Negroes to Miss Crandall's fine female semi-

36

nary. Perhaps at last she'd get an explanation . . .

"Bernadette," David said, "there's something we need to tell you."

She waited. And while she waited — with Hester's face troubled and David looking pointedly over her head — it came home to Bernadette. She wasn't going to hear good tidings. All week she'd puzzled, her wonder laced with foreboding.

"Child, we've no way to send you to school. For weeks we've expected the seminary in Canterbury to put the black girls out and take back the village white girls. But the teacher hangs on to the blacks."

"I don't understand."

"No, of course she doesn't," Hester assured David. "She's hardly talked with a soul since she's come. You see, Bernadette, since the first part of April Prudence Crandall has been headmistress to a school for young women of color."

"But Pastor Fry told me . . ."

"Yes, our brother told you what we wrote him before it all happened."

"And, of course, as Wife has said, we expected every day the schoolmarm would come to her senses and change back to the old school," David broke in. "I still expect it. She'll realize what a mistake she's making, mark my word."

Hester shook her head. "I don't agree that Miss Crandall will give in so easily now. But be that as it may, we owe you an explanation."

Then Hester went on to explain the history of the puzzle. Quaker Miss Crandall was almost thirty years old, had been a respected headmistress in a nearby town. On the strength of fine recommendations, Canterbury's first citizens — Selectman Andrew Judson, Dr. Andrew Harris, Solomon Payne, Isaiah Knight, Rufus Adams — had invited Miss Crandall to Canterbury to establish an exclusive seminary for village girls. The citizens had even made it possible for Miss Crandall to purchase her handsome house. With everyone's favor and backing, the school had opened and been run successfully for nearly two years.

"Then last winter, the teacher took one of her hired help into school as a pupil, a local free mulatto named Sarah Harris," David continued bitterly. "Sarah gave the teacher newspapers and tracts against slavery and before you know it, the headmistress had been converted to this new abolition craze."

Hester took back the tale by describing how in February, when four angry Canterburians had called on Miss Crandall to admonish her for mulatto Sarah's school attendance, Miss Crandall's dry reply had been that since the town threatened to withdraw their white daughters from school because of Sarah, rather than give up black Sarah the teacher would exclude the white students and convert her school to a seminary for free colored females. "Didn't Moses have a black wife?" Miss Crandall had pointedly asked the Scripture-quoting gentlemen.

"But a school just for black girls! Why would she dismiss her own village girls for strange black ones?" Bernadette asked wonderingly.

"Because she's fallen under the spell of a madman and it's unsettled her mind," David Fry declared hotly. "This William Lloyd Garrison with his scandalous new rag, *The Liberator,* advocates freeing the South's slaves right now."

"Garrison's not a madman, David," his wife interposed with gentle insistence.

"He is," David retorted. "Hasn't his rabble-rousing already been responsible for a slave revolt in Virginia where that black renegade Nat Turner killed all the whites he could lay hands on?"

"Garrison's not to blame for that, David."

"Well, the black man had read *The Liberator,* at his trial he admitted he had . . ."

"More's the pity." It was Hester's turn to raise her voice. "After Nat's uprising, white vigilantes ran amok through Virginia killing slaves. They say when the trial was over they boiled Nat Turner's skin for grease . . ."

Shuddering, Bernadette couldn't suppress a wild thought. What color was the grease when it rendered out?

"And now," David accused, "this Garrison gets behind an addle-minded female schoolmarm and brings trouble right to our Canterbury. A female fanatic making a battleground of our village where we've been born and bred; sacrificing our church where we've been christened . . ."

"The change *has* brought bad feelings, Bernadette," Hester admitted. Then she went on to explain how Schoolmarm Crandall, carpetbag in hand, had visited Mr. Garrison in Boston, Mr. Benson in Providence, and Mr. Miller in New York soliciting colored pupils. The combustible Mr. Garrison had spread her story in his *Liberator;* the wealthy abolitionist Tappans of New York stood ready to give her money; Reverend Samuel May of nearby Brooklyn Village had become her staunch ally. But no friends had been gained in Canterbury, where the teacher and the growing number of black students were thoroughly detested. The destruction of the school was the avowed aim of the village.

"So we haven't a place for you to be taught," David finished flatly. "Unless it be at common school."

"But I've gone past what they teach at common school!" Bernadette protested, the finality of the dilemma coming home to her at last.

"We know you're eager and ready for Latin school, but we have nothing we can offer you suitable to your needs," Hester replied softly, taking the baby up over her shoulder and patting it. "That's why I suggest we ask the schoolmistress of the colored school if she would let you study there anyway."

All Bernadette could think of in that first shocked second were the stony, strange profiles of the black girls as they had sat in church. Her next blinding remembrance was of the church folk as they watched the girls and their teacher drummed home.

Of the two images, it was the Negro girls who frightened her more.

"Would you go there if Miss Crandall consented to take you, Bernadette?"

She couldn't find her outer voice, but her inner voice implored, *No, no, don't ask me to go to that school.*

Hearing Hester's proposal, David had whirled from the window and turned a nonplussed look upon his wife. He'd opened his mouth, then shut it and gazed with angry hopefulness at Bernadette instead.

But Hester Fry didn't seem to perceive the feelings of either her outraged husband or stunned Bernadette. She reached over to the candle stand, lifted the oil lamp, and pulled a newspaper from beneath it, a newspaper whose heading was a picture of a slave in chains.

"Mayhap if you look at what Miss Crandall teaches, you'll want to go," Hester said with bright single-mindedness, smoothing out the newssheet on her quilted lap.

Bernadette leaned over and read the words dutifully:

> Prudence Crandall, Principal of the Canterbury (Conn.) Female Boarding School, returns her most sincere thanks to those who have patronized her school, and would give information that on the first Monday of April next, her school will be opened for the reception of Young Ladies and Little Misses of color. The branches taught are as follows: Reading, Writing, Arithmetic, English Grammar, Geography, History, Natural and Moral Philosophy, Chemistry, Astronomy, Drawing and Painting, Music on Piano, together with French Language.
>
> The terms, including board, washing, and tuition, are $25 per quarter, one-half paid in advance.
>
> Books and Stationery will be furnished on the most reasonable terms.

There was no question Miss Crandall's studies could take her back to Oberlin, Bernadette realized with sharp regret.

But as she carefully returned the paper to the table, she rejected what she had found in it. Oberlin or not, every fiber of her shriveled at the thought of going to that school.

"Would you be afraid to go to such a strange school, Bernadette?" Hester asked.

"Yes, I'd be afraid. Not of the townsfolk, but of the girls."

41

"Of the girls? But what could the girls do to you?" Hester cried.

"I'd be uneasy. I've never lived among people of color," Bernadette tried to explain. The baby stirred; Hester handed Rachel to Bernadette to put in the cradle. Bernadette sat down and rocked the cradle with her foot. It was good to sit down because her knees had begun to shake. Besides, rocking might calm the terrified thumping of her heart.

At last, speechless David Fry found his tongue and was galvanized into action.

"Hester, you yourself have imbibed too much of this Garrison. Because of him you've forgotten the way the world is. It'll be untold generations — if ever — before there will be an end to slavery, and you might as well resign yourself to it and think of things more fitting to a female. While you were carrying the child, I humored you, Hester. But now that time is past. There will be no more talk of Bernadette's disgracing us by going to such a school."

Hester finally registered the depth of her husband's feelings. But she did not lack courage.

"And where then do you propose we find a school for Bernadette?"

"School! School! Why does a female need schooling? If Bernadette hasn't yet enough book learning to teach in the country, then she can support herself by the needle."

Bernadette's foot on the cradle paused in its steady beat. The needle? How she'd hate to tuck shirts to keep alive!

"Well, child," Hester finally concluded heavily, "run down and dish up the breakfast. We shan't solve your problem today, I see."

Instead, she ran for her room. She needed time to think

42

by herself, to try to deal with all the feelings that jangled in her.

She just couldn't go to the black school. She didn't know why, couldn't say why. But she just couldn't.

She'd run away to Ohio, that's what she'd do. *I could get there, I know I could.*

But what kind of girl would leave bedfast Hester Fry? What kind of girl would leave the miraculously living baby who needed so much tending?

Besides, what would await her in Ohio? Pastor and all the Frys, yes.

As for Oberlin, so far as she knew, she didn't have enough education to get into Oberlin.

If she fled back to Ohio, Pastor would be disappointed in her. But worst of all, she'd be so disappointed in herself.

She paced the room, stood in front of the wavy mirror, unseeing. She heard a distant cry — the baby was waking. She listened absently.

She could feel a reluctant decision forming in her; it rubbed like sandpaper against her own wants and needs.

She'd stay in Canterbury.

After all, David Fry might be right. The black girls couldn't be permanent where they were hated so much.

She'd have to curb her willful impatience. She knew how hard that would be! Patience had never been her best quality.

Feeling a flinty sort of resignation settling in her, she opened her door, went downstairs. Well, she thought on the bottom step, and not without some saving humor, one way to stand still but get something accomplished was to work.

Paul was still in the kitchen. Hastily, she cut the bread.

43

"They've told you about the school, haven't they? You know who shot that musket?"

"No, I don't."

"Ingo Lewis. He's a good friend of mine," Paul confided unexpectedly. "Those niggers looked like they'd cut and run for their lives if that schoolmarm hadn't been with them."

"I didn't think they looked scared," Bernadette replied shortly, too churned up for tact. Just because she wouldn't go to school with blacks didn't mean she could abide folks being cruel to them.

"Well, I thought the drumming was capital," Paul persisted. "Still, I wish the niggers had never come to Canterbury. I wish my ma didn't read that *Liberator*. For months, she's hardly been able to think of anything but slavery. Pa thought it was just the steriky way she was before the baby came, but she was talking on it again just yesterday. She and my pa don't agree about slavery. They don't agree about Miss Crandall's school either. My ma *ought* not to cross my pa."

Bernadette listened in amazement to Paul's outburst of confidences. You might know if Paul got confidential, it'd be over something Bernadette didn't want to talk about.

It seemed like one thing followed another that day. In the afternoon, when Bernadette carried Hester's plate upstairs, Mrs. Fry was propped against her pillow, looking thoughtful. No doubt thinking about black schools and black slaves, Bernadette guessed.

But Hester spoke of something else, something Bernadette hadn't dreamed she would ever mention.

44

"Dear Bernadette, don't be afraid of what you saw in here." Hester caught Bernadette's hand as it smoothed the sheet.

Involuntarily, Bernadette closed her eyes as though to shut out a picture; her frightened response was not lost on the bedfast woman.

"When your time comes, you'll be ready. To have a child is like sailing a good ship on a broad river, being carried on the current with no need to resist or turn to shore."

Bernadette didn't believe she'd feel like that; she didn't ever want to find out. Others must have the babies, if they would . . .

Since she couldn't make any sense out of what she'd seen, she'd just try to forget.

Hester's eyes looked at her, full of a growing fondness.

Bernadette couldn't bear the look. She took her hand away and, picking up the empty dishes, went out the door.

chapter 5

✝✝✝✝✝✝✝

FRIENDS AND NEIGHBORS dropped in to rejoice over the Frys' healthy baby daughter. Since Bernadette now knew what was afoot in Canterbury, she could make sense of the excited hodgepodge of chatter. What she didn't understand, Hester filled in.

Miss Prudence Crandall had commenced her black school one fine spring day in 1833. On that first day, eggs had been spattered all over the front of the schoolhouse. At the end of the first week, the black girls were taken two by two for a walk. A troop of hooting schoolboys followed them, throwing stones. That night a load of barnyard refuse — feathers, chicken heads, a dead cat — had been deposited on the school's front steps.

Public stage transportation was soon forbidden the girls. A friendly Negro at Norwich risked his business to put his coach at the school's disposal anyway.

In March at the Canterbury Congregational Church, a great public meeting had been held to protest the black school.

"Of course the schoolmarm couldn't appear," Hester informed Bernadette.

"Couldn't appear? But why not?"

"Well, if she'd risked the meeting, she couldn't have spoken anyway. Women can't speak in public, Bernadette."

It jarred Bernadette. She stopped dusting Hester's dower chest and thought back. Could she remember Pastor's lively wife ever speaking up at church meeting? No.

"Why can't women speak out?" she asked Hester Fry.

"Surely you were taught that . . ."

"Everyone worked so hard out there; I guess there wasn't time to teach me everything," she floundered.

"It's in the Bible," Hester replied. "St. Paul said, 'Let your women keep silence.' He said God was the head of man and man the head of woman."

Bernadette revolved the feather duster absently. "Does that seem fair?"

Hester plumped her pillow energetically, not wanting to be diverted. "Well, of course God cursed women through Eve. At least so we're taught back here. But anyway, back to Prudence Crandall. Miss Crandall got Arnold Buffum, an antislavery worker, and Reverend Samuel May of Brooklyn to go to the meeting in her stead."

While Bernadette swept the rug, Hester described the turbulent meeting. Canterbury's most prominent citizen, lawyer Andrew Judson, shouted that Miss Crandall had shown "reckless hostility," town property was no longer safe, and that the school broke down the natural distinction between white and black.

Judson's accusations were typical of others', equally heated.

May and Buffum rose and tried to present a letter from Miss Crandall promising that she would move her school to a less prominent location if the town selectmen would buy her house.

Both men were fiercely shouted down. There were calls of

"Throw them out! Throw them out!" Men of the village surrounded May and Buffum, physically threatened them, and finally hustled them from the church.

The town meeting then passed resolutions against the black school. Till the state could act, Andrew Judson promised to use Connecticut's vagrancy laws against the black girls.

"Under those laws, if a vagrant doesn't move on, he has to pay a fine. If he still doesn't go, he can be striped in public."

"Striped?" Bernadette asked, broom poised in midair.

"Whipped. So many lashes."

"They'd whip the girls?" Bernadette asked, amazed.

"I believe," Hester replied, "they'd do even a thing like that."

Hester brought Bernadette up to date by telling her that five days after the church mass meeting, Judson called on Miss Crandall and personally offered to buy her house — which was next to his own — if she would abandon the school. Sell her house? Yes. But abandon her school? That Miss Crandall refused to do.

By early April, there were twelve pupils at the seminary. On April 1, there was another seething town meeting at the church. The town went on record with charges that the school was a theater at which doctrines of racial intermarriage were promulgated. The pupils had been gathered ostensibly to be taught, but actually to "scatter firebrands, arrows, and death among brethren of our own blood . . . The sentiments the school stands for subvert the union of American states . . ."

The vote at the end of this second meeting requested the Connecticut legislature to pass a law against bringing black people from outside Connecticut for educational or other purposes.

"You saw the drumming after church," Hester finished. "Now the church folk have decided to close their doors against the school, though in the past, we always reserved pews for use of the seminary."

What a broil! Bernadette concluded. Visitors didn't want to talk of anything else, even the lovely baby. Though in bed, Hester stood up against her women friends and condemned the townsfolk as well as the church. That made David Fry angry, ashamed, uneasy. "The teacher will give in," David predicted insistently. Paul grew more morose.

A pox on the black school! Bernadette finally decided resentfully. Whatever its outcome — and however it affected her — for the time being Bernadette was tired of hearing folks rant of nothing else, tired of the strain it put on her new family, tired of trying to keep herself cheerful in the midst of disappointment.

If by the end of June it was this stifling, what would July offer? Bernadette wondered as she tossed and turned in bed, not thinking of the school but instead, of what Hester had said about women. Suddenly the puzzled simmering inside her blazed at the idea of women brazenly being put down, women led not by God but by men.

And how come Pastor had never preached of a hate-filled God who had cursed half of humankind? Even God seemed different back here in Connecticut.

Puzzles like this made it all the more important for Bernadette to find out for herself what the truth was. *I'll learn Greek and Hebrew at Oberlin,* she vowed, throwing off the

quilt precipitously. *Then I can read the true Bible myself, see what it really says.*

She felt better instantly, once her decision was renewed. Hardy optimism — natural to her — flowed through Bernadette. She bounced up, padded in bare feet to her window.

The far-off horizon was splintered by a flicker of lightning. Let's hope a storm comes to break the heat, she thought.

She watched, exhilarated, as great dazzling gashes of light zigzagged down the black sky. How glad she was she didn't fear thunder and lightning! She put her head out the window and relished the rising wind blowing her wild hair.

She looked in the direction of the big tamarack tree next to the house, shut her astonished eyes, and peered again.

Back turned to her, somebody was climbing down the tree!

By another flash, she saw exactly who it was. Paul Fry jumped off a low branch, landed lightly on all fours, picked himself up, and hightailed into the dark!

She nearly yelled, then remembered just in time she mustn't wake anyone.

Where was Paul going at ten o'clock? Someplace mighty fast, she concluded, because he was out of sight like a shot.

But in that last second, before dark had enveloped him, she thought he had glanced over his shoulder and paused momentarily. Had he seen her watching him?

She pulled her head in from the window.

The storm passed over with only a quick spatter of fat drops.

Bernadette climbed into bed. It was some time before she fell asleep.

51

chapter 6

✝✝✝✝✝✝✝

Yesterday was washday. By sunup Bernadette had set an outdoor fire to crackling; by midmorning the tubs of clothes had been stirred, emptied, clearstarched, wrung, and hung to flap in the sun.

Today was ironing day.

She stood in the cavernous kitchen sorting out David's rough-spun overalls, Paul's pantaloons, Hester's bedgowns, her own chemise, the starch-stiff petticoats, and drawers. Out of growing tenderness, Bernadette had folded the baby's flannel nappies first.

She dragged out two straight chairs and set them back to back, then went to fetch the crude wood ironing board to lay across them. Stooping before the hearth, she wet the heavy black flatirons to see if they sizzled.

While she worked, she kept an eye on the ticking Terry clock on the shelf. She'd have to hurry to be finished by noon.

How dull the farm clothes were, she thought, guiding the blunt iron around a blue shirt cuff. The only thing the least bit delightful was Hester's house cap. She worked at its rows of ruching with a diligent protrusion of her tongue, then finally held the cap up in triumph to see how smooth and stiff she'd made it. She liked the cap on Hester — it hugged her broad cheeks and made her plain, friendly face beam out from the ruffles. Well, there was little enough prettiness in a countrywoman's life. Work set its harsh fist on everyone, even here in Canterbury, where things were not so raw as in Ohio.

By noon, Bernadette had started down the lane for Canterbury. Carefully she felt in the pocket of her dress for the shillings Hester had given her. She must get the Bateman's pectoral drops for Paul's congestion, a new milk pail, a tin plate and cup for the table. The chapman's cart, glinting tinware from its sides, had not clanked up the lane recently. So Captain Richard Fenner's Canterbury general store would get their business, Hester instructed.

It was haying time! Bernadette couldn't decide which she liked better — to look or smell. Gazing, she scanned myriad small clouds flecking the summer sky like lambs on a blue meadow. They followed each other over the soft mountain crests in the same single-file way that real flocks followed on the sidehills below.

In the nearby field, a group of men swung their scythes, carving a wide swath in the tall green growth. They worked in beautiful unison, their arms raised and slashing ahead of them. When they came to the end of the row, they put their scythes on end and sharpened them deftly with whetstones. Then they took their places at the beginning of the next lane and the hay fell again before their blades. Cut, it filled the world with fragrance. Bernadette decided she liked the smell of hay-time best.

She ran for the joy of stretching her legs. But when she reached the turnpike she stopped cavorting. Who knew when a peddler's cart, a horseman, or a farmer's wagon might come around the bend? After all, she was fourteen.

53

She skirted the hitching post in front of Captain Fenner's general store. Spitting and arguing, loungers leaned on the porch railing. But when she came up they appraised her in blank, awful silence.

What relief the cool store was! The middle counter was heaped with cloth, the grocery shelves to the right with coffee jars and a grinder, boxes of China tea with strange signs, wood firkins of penny candy. She took a cracker from the cracker barrel, then headed for the shelf where crockery and tinware were stacked. Appreciatively, she sniffed the store's aroma: sperm oil, sage, cheese, piny medicinal balm, hand-rolled cheroots, cider brandy, harness leather, salt codfish . . .

Since the storekeeper was busy selling a farmer a jug of molasses, she had time to decide on the most perfect cup, plate, and pail.

She jumped a mile when the storekeeper asked at her elbow, "You need something?"

"Yes, sir, tinware."

He foraged in his pails. "You stranger in the village?"

"I'm the orphan, Bernadette Savard. I've come to live with the Frys awhile."

After a pause, the Yankee observed in his flat accents, "New baby out there. Fine, healthy girl."

"Yes, sir."

"Mother still getting on well?"

"Yes, sir. She'll be out of bed soon."

"You came east from Ohio, didn't you?"

"Yes, sir. And before that I came south from Montreal."

"French father, isn't that right?"

"Yes, sir," she admitted softly.

54

Captain Fenner really looked at her then, from head to toe, not even pretending he wasn't looking. Bernadette felt a flush start at her throat and go right to the roots of her hair, as the storekeeper catalogued each foreign part of her in his tidy mind.

Before she grew totally flustered, she asked him for the bottle of pectoral drops. They went over to the wall shelf of medicines.

Suddenly the talking on the porch stopped dead. The silence had descended so unexpectedly she glanced out the door.

Footsteps tapped on the porch and a woman's figure appeared against the door light.

With a shock Bernadette realized it was the schoolteacher, Mistress Prudence Crandall. How could she forget the woman who had sat with her black girls in church and led them home in the drumming?

Miss Crandall approached the counter.

Bernadette looked nervously to Storekeeper Fenner. His habitual frosty expression froze into ice before her eyes.

"Captain Fenner, I have an ill pupil. The attack's come on suddenly and I desperately need a bottle of cough medicine." Miss Crandall spoke in a high, clear, you'd-better-mind-me voice.

Captain Fenner said not a word. He just pulled his hand away from the medicine shelf as though it had met with a fire there.

"Captain Fenner, I'm fully aware you've agreed not to sell to me so long as I keep my black school. But this is an emergency; the child suffers from croup and could die."

Deepest silence from the merchant. Over her shoulder,

55

Bernadette realized the doorway was clotted with onlookers.

Up close, Bernadette saw Miss Crandall was a small woman to be standing so stubbornly against the world. Her light brown hair was parted and lay smoothly pulled back over her ears; it was cut short in a businesslike but oddly pleasing style. Her brows were straight and heavy, her intelligent brown eyes steadfast and penetrating. Her nose was too long; her mouth inclined to be wide; her chin was far too square and determined. She wore a neatly laundered blue cambric dress, simple as a countrywoman's.

She's plain and yet not at all plain, Bernadette concluded, not able to put her finger on the elusive, attractive quality about the teacher, reed slim yet doughty, composed yet vigorous.

Reluctant admiration welled up in the girl. Then her admiration mixed suddenly, overwhelmingly, with a choking sense of shame that any human should be forced to beg as Miss Crandall now had to. Bernadette found herself wishing the leering spectators would vanish in a sudden puff of smoke and flinty Captain Fenner be struck down by fires of Lordly wrath.

The silence grew unendurable.

Miss Crandall turned on her heel and walked to the door. The men fell back, gaping.

The schoolmarm passed from view.

After Captain Fenner, grim faced and wordless, had taken Bernadette's coins and handed over her purchases, Bernadette stepped outside into the midst of the pandemonium which had burst out among the loafers.

What a miserable spectacle she had just witnessed!

It didn't matter who was sick, folks should minister to

them. Wasn't that the point of the story of the Good Samaritan? And didn't Storekeeper Fenner rent one of the front pews at church?

She dawdled uncertainly in front of Miss Crandall's house looking up at its windows. Then she glanced at the other nearby houses.

Miss Crandall's chief enemy, Lawyer Judson, lived next to the school in an imposing place. Bernadette studied Mr. Judson's great white clapboard house as if it might offer some clue to the truth of his assertion that Miss Crandall only wanted to educate black girls so they could give themselves airs and marry white boys. Was that what Mistress Crandall intended to do with her girls?

I think it would be a strange white man who'd wed with a Negro girl, Bernadette concluded sagely, despite the Judson house's look of authority. With so many white girls to choose from, why would a young man pick a black one?

As for herself, it would be wonderful to learn astronomy, moral philosophy, and chemistry! But no, not at that black school! Never there! Oberlin would have to be won some other way.

She gave the big schoolhouse a last shuddering glance, then stepped up her pace and rattled with her purchases out of town, a sense of oppression leaving her as Canterbury's huge houses and green yards dropped away.

Down at the bridge a raw-boned, kettle-cut, red-haired boy was taking the tolls. "Where's Paul?" he asked her.

"Paul Fry? He's scything coarse grass in the lower meadow."

"Tell him Ingo said come to town."

"But he can't; he has to work . . ."

"You tell Paul what I said; he'll understand."

She didn't like Master Ingo's looks; he had a troublemaking, fighting-cock air; his pale eyes, which wouldn't focus straight on her, seemed lashless and were capped by white eyebrows.

"I'll tell Paul," she promised shortly.

"What do you have in the pail?"

"A tin cup and plate and a bottle of cough medicine . . ."

Cough medicine! Suddenly the fact dawned on her. She had cough medicine, was carrying away from the village what was urgently needed by a girl gasping for breath with the croup!

Bernadette hurried across the bridge, climbed the hill. She stopped in the road, transfixed, her mind a battleground. Then she walked on again.

But that bottle of medicine belonged to Hester.

Mistress Crandall could borrow medicine from a neighbor — no, none of her neighbors would speak with her. In Canterbury, only Miss Crandall's father, Pardon Crandall, her brothers Hezekiah and Reuben, and her young sister, Almira, came and went from the beleaguered school. And even the father on his farm south of town had urged his daughter to give up.

There was nobody Miss Crandall could turn to.

With war going on in her, Bernadette slowed down. Each dragging step increased her indecision.

It was in this state that she spied two girls clambering up from the creek bed beside the pike.

At first she was so preoccupied she hardly looked at the pair. When she did, she discovered they were brown girls.

Two of Miss Crandall's students were carrying a big sweet-grass basket between them. Probably they were coming straight from Pardon Crandall's farm, which supplied much of the school's food.

Bernadette walked toward them, unaware of decision overtaking her. Instead, she felt fated.

"Please," she breathed, stopping directly in front of them. "I've medicine Mistress Crandall needs."

One girl pushed on, but her companion on the basket handle halted, pulling both of them up short.

"What do you mean?" she asked, fear struggling with curiosity in her face.

"Come along, Ann," the other urged roughly, tugging on the handle.

"Just a minute, Miriam. Let the white girl speak."

Bernadette explained what had happened to Miss Crandall at Captain Fenner's store. "It wasn't till I left Canterbury I realized I had the very medicine your teacher needed. See?" Bernadette reached down and brought out the little bottle from the depths of the pail.

"You're sure you're telling us the truth?" the one called Ann inquired. She spoke well, not at all as Bernadette imagined a black girl would speak.

"It's the truth," Bernadette vowed.

"The medicine isn't even hers to give us," the one named Miriam argued crossly. "She bought it for someone else."

"That's true, but she could let Miss Crandall have it, and Miss Crandall could give her the money to buy more," Ann protested.

"She'll have to come back with us to the school to get her money."

Bernadette thought, *I'll be late getting home.* Still, there was nothing to do but finish what she'd impulsively begun.

The three of them fell in step, two with the basket and Bernadette with her noisy pail.

As she walked, she secretly surveyed both black girls. They were about fifteen, she estimated, though they were no taller than she was. They were shiny brown, and in their sunbonnets and wide-skirted dresses they looked astonishingly alike. Except for their demeanor. The one called Ann had a fawnlike gentleness. But the other, the one called Miriam! She scowled heavily and her eyes flashed; she seemed glittering, fierce, proud. She skimmed along as though carrying a heavy sweet-grass basket were like carrying goose down.

Herself a girl who tried — if she could — to suit people by self-discipline, Bernadette was drawn like a magnet to this reckless, glittery Miriam.

"Do you live hereabouts?" Ann asked.

"I live with the Frys. They have a farm yonder." Bernadette pointed. "Where do you come from?"

Miriam laughed a short, sharp snort. "You can be sure Ann's not from Canterbury. She's had a vagrancy warrant served on her for coming to school from out of Connecticut. If Reverend May hadn't gotten a bond, she'd have been flogged on her bare body, ten stripes."

"Don't talk like that, Miriam," Ann protested. "There's no need to frighten someone who does us a kindness."

"Well, she no doubt knows what the vagrancy law is," Miriam added testily. "She probably agrees the town selectmen should have us whipped."

It rushed out of Bernadette unexpectedly. "No, I don't believe that."

"Well, there aren't many hereabouts like you," Miriam observed ungratefully.

They came to the village boundaries. Bernadette realized she was going to have to walk right up to Miss Crandall's front door with the two colored girls. She remembered the gawking loiterers at the store.

"We can go in the backyard way," Ann suggested. "It's handier." Miriam shrugged knowingly.

The teacher herself opened the kitchen door.

"And who may this be?" she asked when she saw Bernadette.

"She says she has medicine we need," Miriam explained. Awkward, reluctant, Bernadette stepped inside the kitchen.

"You were the girl at Captain Fenner's!" Miss Crandall exclaimed. "You say you've medicine for us?"

Bernadette explained her story.

Miss Crandall's face bloomed with gratitude. "Why, thank you, child! Warm poultices don't seem to help Hattie."

"She'll need money to buy another bottle to take to her family," Ann reminded.

"Of course. I'll fetch some." With an air of distraction, Miss Crandall hurried away.

Surreptitiously, Bernadette inspected the kitchen. It looked like kitchens everywhere — wood floor, high shallow hearth, dish cupboards, a drop-leaf table for mixing dough. From the front of the house, Bernadette heard a babble of girls' voices.

Ann had followed the schoolmistress, and she and Miriam were left alone in the kitchen. Black Miriam with her taunting half-smile fixed steadily on Bernadette's discomfort.

61

They said nothing, divided by a gulf of enormous unknowing.

When she takes off her bonnet, her hair's stiff and brushy, Bernadette observed. Her nose is squashed and her lips stick out. But despite these oddities, Miriam's face held a wild appeal: dark, exotic, with shining high cheekbones and inscrutable, curly-lashed black eyes.

"Would you like to sit down?" the Negro girl asked finally.

"No, thank you. I have to hurry home."

Miss Crandall came back, handed the coins to Bernadette. "What's your name?" she asked.

"Bernadette Savard, ma'am."

"Well, I shouldn't want you to be tardy getting home. Thank you for all you've done," was Miss Crandall's goodbye.

Bernadette looked uncertainly over to Miriam. Miriam bobbed her head stiffly, then smiled. But it was more of a grimace than smile.

It was almost six o'clock when Bernadette arrived at the farm.

"Bernadette, what kept you?" Hester exclaimed.

Tired, dusty, confused, Bernadette told Hester exactly what had happened. Hester didn't scold even when she heard how her coins had been boldly twice spent. She merely told Bernadette to dish up a cold supper of pickles, beans, and smoked ham for David, who was just now coming in from haying.

Bernadette nearly collided with Paul in the hallway.

"A boy named Ingo sent a message to you. He wants you to come to town." Her look was level.

"You saw me shinny down the tree by my bedroom window, didn't you?" Paul asked bluntly. "Will you tell?"

She parried Paul's question. "Where did you run off to, Paul?"

He bristled. "I don't have to tell any girl where I went. Go ahead, tattle on me. It'll just prove you're nebby."

"I'm not nebby!" Bernadette denied, shocked. "Could I help seeing you?"

"No, but you can help tattling. Pox on girls! All they do is mind their elders, and go to bed at night."

"Your pa would thrash you if he knew . . ."

"You'd like that, wouldn't you?" Paul accused. "Miss Stuck-up! Have to go to a fancy school! Girls oughtn't to be schooled anyway; their brains are too feeble for it."

There it was again! Putting women down! In Ohio it hadn't hit Bernadette because of Pastor's cheerful ambitions for her, but putting women down was a raging fever back here, one that threatened to flatten Bernadette personally.

"Girls' brains aren't feeble!" Bernadette nearly shouted. She was about to kick Paul in the shins. Let him bellow!

David Fry called from the kitchen about supper. Bernadette and Paul glared at each other, then she turned and tapped downstairs.

Well, now she knew what Paul Fry thought of her behind all that silence. He considered her nosy, persnickety, stuckup and feeble brained! And a potential tattletale to boot! What a surprising revelation, especially as she'd never intended to tattle about the tree shinnying.

She crashed the kettle lid so hard that from his rocker David gave a startled twitch.

But underneath her indignation, disappointment weighed

Bernadette down. Paul Fry revealed as an enemy — Paul, whom she'd never done anything to.

And no seminary to attend. Her great hopes dimming . . .

She was assailed by a renewed longing for the affectionate Ohio Frys.

She wished she had a friend her own age, at least one.

The dark face of Miriam flashed unaccountably in her mind's eye; Miriam studying her warily . . .

chapter 7

✝✝✝✝✝✝✝

In SLEEPY CONTENTMENT Paul drove the team and wagon down the village street. This bright summer morning he wasn't in the mood to rush home to work.

Rapid hoofbeats sounded behind him. The sheriff and the constable tore around him in a rattling spring wagon. Paul woke up in a hurry as the Fry team jerked nervously crabwise into the grass by the road. Where in tarnation was the law going so fast? Paul wondered irritably as he sawed Herod and Sheba to a halt.

The sheriff's spring wagon drew up in front of Miss Crandall's schoolhouse. The sheriff leaped down. Curiously Paul watched him rap smartly on the front door. A black-faced, brushy-haired girl with round, scared eyes opened up. Almost immediately Miss Crandall, wearing her bonnet and carrying a carpetbag, came to the door.

Wherever she's going, she's been expecting it, Paul guessed. That must be the young sister, Almira, kissing the schoolmarm farewell. The door closed, and with firm steps Miss Crandall marched with the sheriff right in front of Paul's wagon. They crossed the street and began to climb the church hill.

Ansel Bacon pushed his head out the church door, spied the sheriff and schoolmarm as they approached, pulled his head in.

Paul suddenly realized something big must be stirring up at the church. Hastily he leaped from his wagon seat and hightailed up the church green. But at a decent distance from the sheriff and Miss Crandall so as not to appear too nosy.

When Paul slipped into the church, he nearly whistled. The whole civil authority of Canterbury was gathered at the front of the sanctuary. Selectmen clustered around Rufus Adams and Ansel Bacon. All watched like hawks as Miss Crandall and the sheriff marched down the aisle toward them.

Paul leaned against a back wall, reassured to see he wasn't the only curious onlooker. Why, some village folk were plumped right down in the pews!

Hearing didn't do Paul too much good because he had a hard time understanding the parlay that went on between the selectmen and Miss Crandall. To atone for her crimes against the village, he surmised the civil authority expected Miss Crandall to put up something called a bond, otherwise she might have to go to jail.

"But I don't want my patrons to pledge surety for me," Miss Crandall spoke up.

There was a thunderstruck moment, then all the selectmen began to argue with the schoolmarm at the same time. But the stubborn hussy just kept shaking her head and saying she wouldn't put up a bond for herself.

"Then you'll have to be taken to jail and put in a cell like a common felon," Ansel Bacon finally roared, his face as red as a turkey gobbler's.

"Then I must be taken," the schoolmarm answered in a firm voice.

Why was everyone so scared to put her in jail? Paul wondered. If she was going to be so set in her ways, that was by far the best place for her!

The argument ended. Miss Crandall sailed up the aisle, brushing aside the sheriff's proffered arm.

Paul scooted to the door and watched as the teacher and the law returned to the spring wagon and climbed up, the schoolmarm between the sheriff and constable. Without further ado, the sheriff cracked the whip and the horses plunged forward. Wheel spokes turning, the trio bowled off toward the Brooklyn Road.

Paul didn't hesitate a minute. Where was Ingo this morning? He had a mouthful of news to tell him! On the turnpike, the dearborn wagon shook and rattled as Paul slapped Sheba and scolded the canny mare, who hung back in the traces and let the gelding do the running.

Ingo's family were stump-pullers and tollkeepers — it was hard to figure which Ingo would be doing on a morning like this. Paul thought he'd likely be lazing at the tollgate since his pa preferred Ingo's brothers to stump-pull with him rather than Ingo; they got out more stumps, and treated the oxen better, Clarence Lewis declaimed.

Sure enough, Ingo lay stretched out by the tollgate in the shade of a young oak. He was propped, half sitting, half lying, against the trunk, the toes of one dirty foot thrust high in the air, his straw field hat pulled down low. He was whittling.

"Ingo!" Paul shouted.

Ingo compressed himself like an accordion and popped up. "What's happened?"

"Sheriff arrested the schoolmarm, took her to jail in

Brooklyn!" Paul breathed, bringing the team up short by the side of the road.

"Did he?" Ingo asked and just stood there with that considering look growing in his eye. Finally a grin split Ingo's face.

"Won't nobody be with them, then," he finally allowed.

"The sister. I saw her."

"Ah, she's but nineteen." There was a pregnant pause. "Why don't you come by tonight, Paul?"

"You shouldn't have told Bernadette to ask me to come to town," Paul complained. "She saw me the other night. From now on it'll be harder to get away."

"She tell on you?"

"Not so far," Paul answered uneasily. "But I'm not sure if she mightn't. She's a girl; she tries not to do forbidden things."

"You're not afraid of a girl, are you? You know, I figgered a way to get in that schoolhouse."

Looking down at Ingo, Paul realized the things his friend said made him increasingly uneasy — all this talk of getting in the school, most of all. Plastering the walls with eggs and dumping rotten stuff at the doors was one thing, but this other?

"Come by tonight. We'll do somethin' big," Ingo promised, very cool. He lifted the tollgate; Paul had been to the mill and didn't need to pay.

Paul rattled off, lost in thought. Ingo and his friends weren't like the academy boys; that's why Paul had first wanted to join up with them. They didn't care a rap what the minister said; they didn't give a fig for school books, either. Paul didn't like school — couldn't see how it would help him run a farm — but he squirmed at some of the things Ingo chuckled over. Like the black schoolgirls, for instance.

Paul shared the view of the village about the brushy-haired girls. In themselves, they didn't interest him. They weren't worth all the trouble they caused. Even if they were free Negroes, what were free Negroes but the result of careless ownership? And slave or free, what did it matter? Blacks didn't have the sense whites did, never would. They were enslaved by a righteous ancient curse; it was as simple as that.

But Ingo's snickering bubbled into Paul's mental dialogue; he finally let it well up in helpless fascination. Ingo wanted to tear up school books, spill ink, snap quills. He wanted to get right at the black girls' things — swipe shawls and bonnets, trinkets. Ingo had said he'd like to chase those girls from room to room, scare them pea green. Paul's skin crawled when Ingo had suddenly remarked, "Niggers are s'posed to smell different than white folks, did you know that?"

Paul wished he hadn't remembered these things. Down deep, he thought the devil writhed in Ingo, that's what. He didn't want the devil to writhe in *him*.

Suddenly he noticed the sun was at midmorning high. He'd have to make tracks if he were to get the hen-house boards cut and ready for nails. Also, it occurred to him his mother might like the news of Mistress Crandall; his status as bearer of dramatic tidings spurred him on.

He careened up the lane, the new lumber jumping and crashing in the wagon bed behind him. "Whoa! Whoa!" he commanded as he circled the barnyard. "Mother! Ho, Ma!"

Hester looked out the door. Behind her on the table, mounds of garden peas waited shelling and immersion in steaming hearth water. She came to the stoop. "What's the matter with you, Paul?"

Paul hopped down from the wagon; when they hit the ground, his bare feet sent up a puff of dust. He catapulted into the kitchen.

"They've arrested her!" he announced.

"Arrested who?" Hester asked.

"The schoolmarm. I saw it."

"Prudence Crandall?" Hester exclaimed, unbelieving.

"I saw the sheriff and constable cart her off to jail in Brooklyn," Paul affirmed importantly.

"That's the end of the black school, isn't it?" Bernadette asked. Paul glimpsed pure relief on the young questioner's face.

"I expect so." Hester sighed. "Miss Crandall can't run a school from jail."

Then, as Paul watched, Bernadette's face clouded over uncertainly. "But why would they arrest her?"

"It must be because of the new black law. Last month in the Assembly at Hartford, the legislators openly admitted they were going to destroy Miss Crandall's school. They raised their fists when they passed the new law against her and said that if it wasn't enough they'd write another."

"What law was that?" Paul asked.

"Well, you know — the one everyone's talking about. The one that says no Negro can come from out of Connecticut to be educated in our schools. Since Miss Crandall's girls are recruited from Boston, Providence, even New York, naturally that's the surest way to get at her."

70

"What will happen to the black girls?" Bernadette asked thoughtfully.

"If they jail the teacher, I don't see how the young sister can manage the school for long. She's too young. Though I believe there's a young man helping now."

"Pa says they should just pack the nigger girls home. Why don't you agree, Ma?" It occurred to Paul his mother might have some sensible reasons for her growing aversion to slavery, ones he'd not heard before.

But, no, it turned out his ma didn't have a sensible answer, just the same old tiresome ones. His ma disagreed with his pa about the Colonization Society, which declared the way to solve slavery was — little by little — to settle the blacks back in Africa. Mr. Garrison, his ma said, pooh-poohed the Colonization Society because it had so far sent back only a trickle of blacks to Africa, never could send very many. Besides, his ma claimed most of them didn't want to go back to their jungle.

His ma fell silent, her face a study. Paul stood on one foot and then another, wondering what she was thinking. He wished she could really explain to him how she'd picked up this abolition fever.

How could Hester explain what had become almost an instinct in her? On this hidden hillside, how had the world's winds of change been perceived, embraced by her? How had she sensed that in 1833 there was a miracle in human history unfolding? That the separate faces of men were standing out from the mass wherein they lived. That despotism trembled in Latin America, tottered violently in France, eroded in England. That tyranny of government was diminished by the demands of sailors flogged at sea,

71

debtors locked in jail, frontiersmen without money to pay the poll tax, indentured bogtrotters on the western canals — yes — even the madman in his chains. Hester knew that the black slave, too, had a separate face: after much thinking, she had joined his scattered, firebrand friends.

"Abolitionists want to free slaves right away, isn't that right?" Bernadette spoke up in her soft voice.

"Yes, they do. And they've agitated so successfully in England, the British are commencing to free slaves in the West Indies by purchase this summer."

"Couldn't ever happen in our country," Paul pronounced with finality. "There's proof in the Bible a slave's meant to be a slave."

"There are other things in the Bible which say the opposite, Paul," his ma answered sharply. "If you'd only read *The Liberator* . . ."

"I don't care for blacks," was Paul's reply. "And there's too much farm work for reading newspapers."

"If it's work that keeps a body from reading, I should hardly know how to trace the alphabet," Hester retorted.

Further news of Miss Crandall was borne to them that afternoon by Neighbor Shaw when he rode by to leave mail. Paul and David came in from their hen-house nailing to hear Neighbor Shaw.

It seems as soon as the sheriff and Miss Crandall had come to Brooklyn jail, Miss Crandall's crony, Reverend May, had been sent for. The sheriff naturally had expected May would insist on posting bail for the stubborn teacher.

"But, no," Neighbor Shaw recounted dramatically, "the

pair of them wouldn't miss a chance to get their names in the newspapers and disgrace our village. With both refusing to scratch up bail, of course the schoolmarm had to be bolted into a cell."

"I hope she stays there till she learns some sense," Paul's pa observed ungallantly.

"She's likely to learn some sense from this cell," Neighbor Shaw opined. "It's the one Oliver Watkins was put in the night before he was hanged."

"The one murdered his wife?" David asked, amazed.

"The same," the old farmer answered. "I don't hold with this black-school ruckus, but I don't know as they needed to put a lady in a cell like that! Still, I reckon it'll make a flaming headline."

After supper, Paul sprawled down beside Bernadette on the stoop. "Looks like the niggers and the schoolmarm are done for," he observed affably.

"Yes," Bernadette answered thoughtfully. "I want a white school to start up so I can go to it, I want it in the worst way. Still, shutting the schoolmarm in jail seems terrible to me. And I've been thinking. After all, what's she trying to do? Just give some poor girls their chance, girls who wouldn't get one any other way."

"But they're nigger girls."

"I don't know, Paul," Bernadette responded soberly. "Black girls or not . . ." Then she sighed. "Well, I'm all mixed up." And with that she flounced off the stoop and ran up toward the orchard.

Paul watched her go. She seemed to do a lot of her thinking in the orchard, he observed.

Even to him there was something appealing about the young girl's running. Be awful to be an orphan, Paul realized suddenly.

Then he thought no more about Bernadette. He whittled, and felt good that the school in Canterbury was over. It had certainly been a terrible mess while it lasted. Some of it fun, though. He wondered idly whom Ingo would think of to pick on next.

The day after, Paul was disgusted all over again. After the schoolmarm had spent a night in jail, yellow Reverend May had posted bond for her after all. She'd come home to her school. The law had to let her stay there waiting trial for breaking the new black legislation. Stay there to run her school. And the night of imprisonment would spread her name, spread it even out of Connecticut.

Out of jail and a martyr to boot, Paul recognized angrily. He went into town to talk with Ingo.

chapter 8

✝✝✝✝✝✝✝✝

Bᴇʀɴᴀᴅᴇᴛᴛᴇ ᴋɪᴄᴋᴇᴅ a new piece of wood beneath the three-legged pot. Chowder bubbled.

She felt bubbly herself because in her pocket she carried a letter from Pastor Fry. Magically, her mood had lightened; Pastor always made everyone feel good things were about to happen.

She sat down in the kitchen rocker and read her letter again. Pastor Fry wrote in a bold, exuberant script with a fine disregard for commas and periods and a fondness for dashes.

Dear Bernadette,

Mother Fry, the girls, Jonathan, and his rascally brothers send their love to you — By now you have settled in with David, Hester, Paul, and the new baby, Rachel — Our prayers have been answered and Rachel thrives — What joy you must be to Hester though her joy is our sorrow — Mother says she misses your merry brown eyes and willing ways and I miss someone who likes to conjugate! No one asks me questions anymore — It is very humbling to live with such a knowing tribe! Jonathan says you must not care for Paul Fry as much as you care for him.

We know you are anticipating entering Miss Prudence Crandall's seminary next term. David wrote that she was trained at Friends Boarding School in Providence and that she had once had a fine school at nearby Plainfield. I hope you will learn moral philosophy — You must memorize pages of Paley, dear Bernadette, and don't ask Miss Crandall too many questions about it — In time it will be clear to you.

Our news? Well, let me see — Ruth fell down the cellar steps with a pan of potatoes and hash and in trying to get up overturned a barrel of soft soap all over herself! Jonathan was late yesterday to empty the wash tub — He says it was Mr. O'Connor's fault for keeping him after school — Jonathan will never believe his sins belong to himself. In the church, we have two new families who walk through the woods to services — All of four miles!

I've been back to Oberlin College — It looks much improved, my dear child! About 20 acres of trees have been chopped, so you can see a college square — A half-dozen houses are in the building stage — they'll be painted red because it's cheaper — won't that light the woods! Streets are opening up but aren't yet thrown or ditched — The road from Elyria is still a dense track, however.

Four acres have been planted to grain and edibles and are really cleared — However, college square is still not stumped and a person could jump from stump to stump all the way across it to class.

Oberlin Hall half stands at the corner of Main and College Streets — It will have a boarding hall, chapel, meeting room, schoolrooms, professors' quarters, and private little rooms for 40 students, 20 of them to be men in the attic! For 4 cents an hour the girls are to help earn their education by doing the boys' laundry and mending — thread that hated needle, brown-eyes! The college will charge 75 cents a week for a vegetable diet, $1.00 for meat twice a week — For a 40-week school year it will cost $60 to $90. So you see, your Uncle Marcus is prepared to be very generous, Bernadette.

Haying is a busy time — There is cholera at Cincinnati — It is bad in Reverend Lyman Beecher's new seminary — The talk is all against slavery down there.

Little sister, write us your news and especially your progress at school —

May you remain in Christ's care,
Robb Fry

Bernadette folded the letter, put it back in her pocket thoughtfully. What would she say to Pastor Fry about Canterbury's female school? That Hester Fry could find no solution? That David Fry insisted girls didn't need fancy schooling? That Paul — oh, Paul's accusations were sore in Bernadette still!

Did Pastor believe in the Bible's cursing of women? What would Pastor feel about one white girl going to school with all blacks?

In the worst way she wanted his counsel, advice. But she was beginning to feel she was childish. She needed to solve her problems herself.

The baby in her cradle was unusually still. Bernadette tiptoed over to peer in curiously.

77

Rachel's deep-blue, heavy-lashed eyes — so calm and reassuring — found Bernadette's look. There was an instant's hesitation, then a tremulous smile lit up the beautiful little face.

Rachel's first smile! And for her, Bernadette!

Bernadette gathered up the baby, held her against her shoulder. Trustingly the little body snuggled close, the little face nuzzled her neck.

A rush of tenderness filled Bernadette; for the first time she realized how strong her feeling for Rachel was. She thought she would burst with love.

Hester entered the kitchen and nodded understandingly.

"*Alive?*" Hester, the mother, had asked.

"*Thank God!*" Hester had whispered.

For the first time, Bernadette dared to remember Rachel's beginning.

What could be remembered, could it one day be accepted?

chapter 9

ψψψψψψψ

Bernadette knew the shortcuts to town by now. Her trip had better be fast.

The basket on her arm was loaded with kitchen-garden vegetables. After she'd delivered them to Miss Crandall she'd tell Hester what she'd done. Hester would understand.

Bernadette had really felt outrage when she'd heard Pardon Crandall had been ordered away from his daughter. Maybe an orphan would just naturally sympathize because an orphan would understand the penalty of being forbade a father.

Yes, Miss Crandall's Quaker father had been ordered by the constable not to bring the school any supplies from his farm. By an act of legislature, Pardon Crandall would be fined one hundred dollars for the first visit and two hundred for any subsequent visits.

The church was now barred against the school; Dr. Harris wouldn't attend its sick; and the local butcher, milkman, and greengrocer refused Miss Crandall service. It must be small comfort to the schoolmarm to have a few loyal friends all the way over in Brooklyn and Packerville. They were too far away to help with the constant necessity of eating!

As she climbed to the turnpike Bernadette glanced the length of the gray stone road and saw in the distance a trunk peddler stooped under his burden. She wondered what notions he offered for sale in his battered tin trunk: probably scissors, razors, pins, and needles.

All of a sudden, something moved in the underbrush at the roadside and startled her. Maybe a farm animal strayed from its pasture. Then she heard shouting. The brush grew still; its agitated leaves stopped rustling.

Something strange must be hidden in there. Bernadette paused warily.

Up onto the pike burst the running figure of a boy. Three more came pelting after him. They were big lads, Paul's age.

"She's hid somewheres!" their leader shouted. "Look in the brush!"

Why, Bernadette knew him! That was Paul's friend, Ingo Lewis.

Boys shot in all directions; one almost ran right over her. They burrowed into the dense greenery.

"She's here!" She heard a triumphant shout.

Bernadette couldn't believe her eyes at what followed. Flushed from its hiding place like a woods animal, came a bonneted girl, her skirts blowing in the wind made by her running. As she came up on the road, not an arm's-throw from Bernadette, her sunbonnet slid back from her head and revealed her face: it was Prudence Crandall's Miriam.

"Miriam!" Bernadette exclaimed as the girl flew by.

Miriam crossed the road and dived off into the woods on the other side. There were *halloos* from that direction; her way had been cut off.

The black girl whirled and started up the open road toward the village. At once Ingo dashed forward to block her escape. Miriam turned and without a moment's hesitation ran straight back toward Bernadette. Her face wore an expression of pure terror.

"Miriam!" Bernadette screamed and dropped her basket to try to catch the girl. They crashed to the road together in a tangle of skirts and tumbling vegetables.

Miriam scrambled up, making no sign of recognition, intent only on getting to the open road whch lay behind.

Bernadette struggled to her feet, dazed, seeing the boys run to close off the black girl's exit. In numb horror she heard exultant shouts and saw the first stone hurled.

"At her!" one yelped. Rocks rained down on the Negro.

As they struck, Miriam stopped, stood still for a second, then dropped to her knees. Her head bowed down, finally she covered it with her arms. Then she leaned forward on the road so that only her back was exposed. Her wide green skirts spread out around her.

Anger consumed all Bernadette's fear. She had never seen a person tormented so.

"Stop that, Ingo Lewis!" she screamed.

The boys were too excited. They ignored her.

"Hit the nigger girl!"

"Go home, black witch!"

Other words defiled the air, words Bernadette burned at hearing.

She scraped frantically at the turnpike and came up with a handful of pebbles. She threw as fast and as far as she could, stooped, scraped, threw again.

The trunk peddler! Where was the trunk peddler? She looked around wildly and spied him.

81

A short way off, he sat on his tin trunk watching.

She raced to him. He observed her through sharp eyes in a bearded, gritty face.

"Help her!" she implored. "Please help her!"

"Calm yourself, gal, I been to the South. Them niggers only good for cotton chopping."

"They'll hurt her."

"Bruise or two won't matter. Won't show."

"She's not a slave. She's freeborn," Bernadette pleaded.

"She's a slave for all that," the peddler retorted. "All of them's slaves . . ."

Nonetheless, he finally got up, and in the most laconic manner ambled over to stand near the prone body of the girl.

"Say, boys, quit now! You've had your sport," he bawled, ducking a missile.

"Git away. Git away!" Ingo shouted.

"I'll fetch the tollkeeper," the peddler yelled. "Scat now!"

"Aw, c'mon, Ingo! He'll fetch your pa."

"We skeered her enough so's when she gits up she'll run all the way to New York," another said.

Reluctantly Ingo's poised arm lowered. Then quick as a flash, the whole crew of rowdies jumped from the road's edge and followed Ingo into the brush.

Bernadette stooped over Miriam.

"Miriam!" she cried, shaking her shoulder. "Get up. They're gone."

Slowly Miriam's head came up. She looked around in terror, then rose to her feet. Before Bernadette could detain her, a last burst of frenzy propelled Miriam toward the woods.

Bernadette hesitated only a second before she went after Miriam. From the turnpike, the peddler watched the girls

disappear. He glanced up at the cloud-choked sky, shrugged, and lifted his trunk to his shoulder.

Running, Bernadette nearly tripped over Miriam, who had collapsed just inside the green brush.

She knelt beside Miriam, pulled her shoulder back, and looked into the still face. Hot tears fell on that upturned face.

Miriam's eyes opened. They peered at one another dumbly.

"Can you walk to my house?" Bernadette whispered.

Miriam stirred, mumbled, finally half sat, shaking her head. "I don't know," she answered with great effort.

Bernadette helped her up. "Come on." She felt the welts that rose on Miriam's shoulders. There seemed to be bleeding through the green cloth.

The kitchen door had been shut against a sudden summer squall.

A faint scratching noise brought Hester from the brick bake oven to the door. As she threw it open, she backed away from the gust of rain which blew in.

Soaked to the skin, Bernadette stood on the sill supporting a strange, dark, drooping figure.

"Boys stoned her," was all she gasped.

Between them, they got Miriam to the big settle which faced the fireplace. While the baby fussed in her cradle and hissing food dripped into the fire from the burning pot on the crane, Hester and Bernadette worked silently over the Negro girl.

chapter 10

⊹⊹⊹⊹⊹⊹⊹⊹⊹

It poured all night. Fuming wordlessly, Paul took the black gelding and galloped to the village to tell them at the seminary what had become of Miriam Hosking. He felt sick to his stomach from his view of the black girl's bruised face, from his guilty suspicion of how it must have happened. Resentful of Bernadette for bringing the "black thing" to roost in his home, he hid out in the barn till time for bed. There he smoked sullenly on the tobacco leaf he'd swiped from his father's backyard patch.

In the kitchen, David sat stiffly before the fire, his pipe cold, his thoughts long. He listened intently for sounds from upstairs.

Miriam lay in Bernadette's bed. Hester and the girl hovered beside it. Studying the black girl, Bernadette tried to relate this helpless Miriam to the Miriam with the sweet-grass basket. That Miriam had worn the iron air of one without frailty, of one who would guard her soul with jealous intensity, would lay it bare grudgingly and seldom in its entirety.

But delirium was stripping defenses away; shock was exposing self. As evening wore on, Miriam began to speak jerkily.

"White girl?"

"Yes. I'm Bernadette."

"You know those stone-throwing white boys?"

"One of them," Bernadette admitted. "Ingo Lewis, the tollkeeper's son."

"A village truant, a liar, a bully . . ." Hester added quietly.

"White girl?"

"I'm Bernadette."

"Bernadette," Miriam muttered, "did you feel sorry for me?"

"Of course I did."

There was a long silence, then a little clicking noise commenced — Miriam's teeth were chattering. Hester went to fetch more blankets.

"In Rhode Island my grandmother lives with us. She knows about us. I'm Coromantee, part of me; what part is not Foulah . . ."

"What does Coromantee mean?"

Hester Fry returned, arms loaded with wool quilts. Bernadette tucked the cover under Miriam's chin. Little by little the clicking noise subsided.

Next door in her cradle Rachel began to fuss. Once more Hester left, this time to tend the baby.

"Gold Coast," Miriam suddenly burst out, half sitting up. "From a port called Cormantyn. Anybody in Jamaica knows where Coromantees come from."

"I'm sorry," Bernadette apologized. "I've never been to Jamaica."

Miriam thrashed feverishly. "Coromantee niggers led many revolts in Jamaica. They don't like to work fields; they fight. Some sellers of slaves grew afraid of my people, wouldn't ship them, wouldn't buy them. But others would

86

buy nothing else, would pay highest prices for them — others who wanted courage, wanted a friend more than a slave. Some said there was never a rascal or a coward called Coromantee. What were your people?"

Bernadette was struck speechless by the sudden question. Her people? Those shadowy, always hunted faces which eluded her? "Well, my mother's father was Captain Gray, a ship's captain in the American navy. He lived in Oswego, in New York state, and my mother and father met there when my father came over from Canada to buy traps."

"Traps?"

"My father was a trapper with the Hudson's Bay Company. His name was Émile Savard. His father and grandfather once lived on a farm on the St. Lawrence River."

"So how was it you came to be here, far away?"

"My father was lost in the northern wilderness and my mother coughed herself . . . my mother died. My old great-uncle in Ohio brought me from Montreal to America when I was young."

"Ah," Miriam breathed, "you were brought. Did you want to be brought?"

"I'm not sure. I don't remember," Bernadette answered in confusion.

"Probably you didn't," Miriam concluded knowingly. Her eyes flickered open, surveyed Bernadette fleetingly, shut tightly again. "People don't like to be brought; they like to come of their own accord."

Hester carried the baby into the room. It was a comfort to Bernadette when Hester handed Rachel to her. The baby made Bernadette forget about the white northern snows which haunted her dreams, made her forget the half-memories of a mother's hand, a mother's voice, a smile . . . made her forget a mother's coughing.

Bernadette's attention returned to the dark face on the white pillow. She was surprised to find Miriam watching her.

"Grandmother's sixty-five," Miriam whispered confidingly. "She was Beeljie, the Foulah. In Africa, she lived in the plain of Timbo where there were big plantations and rice fields. Grandmother said Timbo village had high stake walls around it and inside everyone was busy, the women with spinning wheels and the men working leather and iron. Or reading and writing."

"Reading?" Bernadette asked, amazed.

"Foulah are Mussulmans," Miriam answered irritably. "They read the Koran, the Mussulman's Bible. They were themselves hardly ever taken into slavery, their walls were so dense, their men so brave."

"How did it happen your grandmother was sold then?"

"She was just sold, that's all. In Jamaica — before Grandma Beeljie was brought to this country — she found my grandfather, the Coromantee. They were lucky; they were shipped north together."

Hester rose and wrung out a rag in the bowl. "Fetch the camphor after you put the baby down," she instructed Bernadette softly. "I must get Miriam to stop talking; she should sleep."

Hester lifted Miriam from the pillow and nodded to Bernadette to bring the basin and towel. The bedgown was slipped from the shoulders and the swollen back revealed. The two of them sponged carefully, especially where the flesh was cut.

How magnificent the skin was, Bernadette thought abruptly. It seemed to glisten in the candlelight with a kinetic mystery. Her own arm beside it looked pallid, dull, weak. She was amazed at what she thought.

"In Carolina . . ." Miriam whispered hoarsely, struggling.

"You must rest," Hester ordered. Miriam's half-closed eyelids trembled; the eyes glimmered beneath them. They seemed to share a last unspoken confidence with Bernadette. Later . . . later . . . they said.

Hester went to her chair. Bernadette curled up carefully on the foot of the bed. Hester's face was drained and gray. She sat for a time, saying nothing; then exhaustion overcame her. Her chin slipped down and she slept.

It was earliest morning, dull and sodden. Bernadette was roused, more by Miriam's quietness in the bed than by any twisting and turning. She raised herself up on her elbow and saw that Miriam was staring out the window. Hester still slept in the chair, her cap awry.

"How do you feel?" Bernadette whispered.

Miriam stretched in a tentative way. "I'm stiff and sore."

"The swelling on your face has gone down," Bernadette observed.

She lay back, thought of the breakfast fire which must be lit. She'd never have the strength to set it nor do a day's work afterward.

Something washed gradually into her mind. She rose up on her elbow again. "Miriam, what happened to your grandmother when she came to this land?"

Miriam shot her a dry, closed look, a look which admitted

that in those vulnerable hours of misery she might have spoken too much, shared too many things of herself.

"Why," she replied sardonically, "my grandmother was a slave and mate to a slave, and both were sold together to a Rhode Island man. In Rhode Island, the slaves lived in the master's dirt cellar — men, women, and children together. My grandfather went blind and grew too old to work, so they turned him out to wander in the woods. But eventually Rhode Island freed its slaves and my mother didn't have to sleep under the bed in her master's chamber anymore. She lives with my father, a free Negro in Providence and a fine comb maker, and my sister and I know how to read and cipher. I've come up here to be stoned on your fine Connecticut road. Have I left out anything else you must know?"

The sarcastic rebuff angered Bernadette. She looked hard at Miriam. "You don't have to be that way with me, Miriam," she warned quietly. "Not after last night."

"I saw you stare at us in church as though we were animals in a cage," Miriam flared.

Bernadette knew it was true. She *had* looked at the black girls that way. But she hadn't yet had this experience with Miriam; she hadn't yet had the chance to discover a person was hiding inside that skin.

The *real* Miriam had been born for Bernadette last night . . .

"I looked at you that way because you were strange to me," Bernadette retorted honestly. "How does Miss Crandall look at you?"

"As though she seeks something to improve," the dark girl answered shrewdly. "Still, she's kind and brave."

Bernadette understood those canny words — old Great-

Aunt Gray's improving glance came to mind. It seemed there was something alike in Miriam and herself; she tried to decide what it was. Thinking deeply, Bernadette closed her eyes and slipped away into drowsy oblivion.

When she awoke, Hester had come to life. She was bending to examine Miriam's cuts, her hands probing gently.

"Do you feel well enough to ride to town in the buggy, Miriam?" Hester asked.

"Yes, ma'am. They must be very upset with me at the school."

Bernadette climbed off the bed and stumbled to the dower chest where she found a clean chemise and petticoat for Miriam. She handed them to the girl; then, rumpled and drowsy-eyed, she left to set the fire.

Breakfast was silent. When Miriam entered the kitchen, David and Paul acknowledged her presence by awkward nods and followed these by just enough conversation to keep the rich milk for their mush passing. Bernadette was grateful for the noise of the snapping hearth, the baby's rapt gurgles from the cradle — even the burst of rain which suddenly pelted the water-gray window. Miriam kept her eyes on her plate.

"We'll need Sheba hitched to the chaise, Paul. You're to take Miriam to town this morning. Don't you think Bernadette should ride with them — Miriam's been so mistreated?" Hester asked David anxiously.

"If you can spare her," the husband replied somberly. "Good-bye, Miriam; I hope your wounds improve," was all he added as he left the kitchen and its charged atmosphere.

Paul mopped his syrup with a hurried hand, kicked back his chair, took his hat from the door peg, and fell onto the stoop. Bernadette guessed what was troubling Paul. He'd have to parade right through the village streets with a Negro. That Ingo would probably heap ridicule on Paul.

Hester bade Miriam a warm farewell. Miriam offered no words but her expression was one of open gratitude, very different from the veiled glance David had earned.

Pulling the buggy, Sheba splattered water back on them; once Miriam wiped muddy spray from her face. Bernadette looked more closely at her by light of day. One eye was smaller than the other, one cheek still swollen. Miriam's bedraggled sunbonnet tried to hide her hair, but a stiff wisp poked straight out like an Indian's forelock. Suddenly Bernadette felt both the urge to laugh and to hug this Miriam who looked so forlornly funny. She dared to put a hand on the hunched-over shoulder.

At the touch, Miriam gazed bleakly at Bernadette, and at last her need for closeness stripped her wholly bare. "I wish I could go home," she whispered.

I wish I could go home!

How many times Bernadette had prayed the same thing! *Oh, Miriam, that's another thing we share, that dream.*

What else did they share?

"But if you went home what would you do there?"

"I promised to teach my sister what I'm learning and teach the girls of my church, too."

And I? I'm a girl, but I'm going to Oberlin Institute in Ohio. I promised Pastor Fry. I promised myself. Most of all, I'm beginning to feel like I've promised other girls, too — a lot of them. Besides, I don't want to live from place to place, beholden to folk.

"If I'm to teach my sister, I can't go home," Miriam finally

93

decided, shrugging. Then she straightened, but not before a helpless shrug, a droll sigh, a different gesture. Did Miriam appeal to her from beneath the fierceness? Was there laughter, warmth, softness?

Head ducked down, Paul trotted the chaise as fast as he could to the teacher's front-door stoop. There he sawed on the bit till the horse stopped, then sat motionless, waiting for Miriam to climb out.

I'm not going to let her get down alone from the buggy. The decision popped out of Bernadette.

Miriam spoke softly out of the corner of her mouth, "Do you know North Hill? I often hike there midweek in late afternoon. You can see from there into Rhode Island."

"I'll find it," Bernadette breathed, then climbed down and waited for Miriam to follow her.

The dark girl rose, swayed, reached out a hand for the chaise's dasher handle to steady herself. Then she crumpled to the seat and fainted.

"Paul!" Bernadette cried in alarm.

Paul seemed at a total loss. But at last it must have dawned on him that if he was to be delivered of his horrid burden he'd have to carry it away himself.

The boy poked one hand under a shoulder and grappled among the green skirts with the other. He lifted Miriam, all bunched in his arms, and jumped to the ground.

A young woman stood at the door, one who looked like Prudence Crandall, except younger and more worried.

"She's only fainted," Bernadette hastily explained, seeing the young sister's alarm.

"Mr. Burleigh is gone this morning," Almira Crandall replied, "and my sister is unwell. Would you lay Miriam on the kitchen settle?"

They hurried down the hall, several black girls trotting behind them.

Paul put Miriam on the settle as though she were a meal bag. He would have instantly escaped the place, Bernadette knew, but by now girls squeezed all around them. She noticed stolen, sidelong stares.

Almira bathed Miriam's face. Finally Miriam stirred; her eyes opened. She looked up at that circle of curious onlookers.

"Do you feel better?" Miss Almira asked anxiously.

"Yes, ma'am."

"Miriam, we've been so concerned. How did you get out of the house unnoticed yesterday?"

Miriam shrugged, said nothing.

"Why did you go out alone, Miriam?"

Another maddening shrug.

"Miriam," the young teacher warned, "you know it's against the rules to go out without permission. You know we can't keep students who don't mind our rules, or once they've broken them, refuse to explain."

Miriam struggled to sit up, thought better of it, and lay back, her face brooding. Finally she whispered, "I went to look for her . . ."

Almira looked full at Bernadette.

"The girl who found you on the road?" the teacher asked incredulously. "Why would you seek her?"

Miriam lay still, and Bernadette sensed how total was the black girl's humiliation. "She was kind to Ann and me about the cough medicine. I wanted to find her."

Almira turned to the astonished Bernadette. "We live in a prison here," she explained matter-of-factly. "We have friends but none close by. For a rover like Miriam it's especially hard. Perhaps she couldn't make herself believe that in all Canterbury there wasn't someone who didn't hate us or wish us ill."

"I don't wish you ill," Bernadette protested. "As a matter of fact, I was bringing kitchen-garden vegetables to you when I met Miriam and the boys on the road. I know your father, Pardon Crandall, was forbid by the law to help feed you."

"He comes anyway," Almira Crandall said simply. "Still, my sister and all of us thank you for helping Miriam. Our hearts go out to you for that kindness. And for the thought of the vegetables, too."

By now Paul had worked his way to the outer ring of girls. He kept wagging to Bernadette with urgent nods of his head.

Bernadette was too flustered to say more, even to Miriam. Outside seemed less complicated. It was good to escape outside.

She followed Paul to the chaise and climbed up.

And then outside didn't seem so simple after all. Caring for a person could be a puzzling thing, she was deciding. Also, caring could bloom from unlikely seeds: a bitter glance exchanged in church could grow unaccountably into Miriam's just-uttered admission of need, a need Bernadette knew was a mutual need.

Yes, Bernadette, too, had been longing for a close friend in this lonesome new place. And now black Miriam had held out her hand as that friend . . .

The final hesitant puzzle still lay in herself.

chapter 11

✤✤✤✤✤✤✤✤

"WHERE'S FATHER?" Paul demanded when they came into the kitchen.

"Waiting for you to turn the wheel while he sharpens the scythes," Hester answered, looking up curiously.

"Bernadette was taking our kitchen-garden vegetables to the Crandall school when the nigger was stoned," Paul accused.

"Wait, Paul!" Hester Fry called after him. But she was too late — the door had already slammed behind her son.

Hester turned to Bernadette, who stood filled with consternation. "Never you mind, child. I'll explain to David you meant no harm. But next time ask me before you do such a thing."

The words were hardly out of her mouth when David entered, his face uncommonly stern.

"Wife, you're to blame for this. You've led the girl astray with your interest in abolition and your sympathy for the schoolmarm's school."

"I'm not sorry for what I believe," Hester replied staunchly. "Still, if my beliefs have made trouble for Bernadette, well, then, I'm sorry because I love her. I don't think what she did deserves punishment, David. She went with a generous heart."

"Generous heart, yes, but with other folks' belongings and without permission."

Bernadette sat down on the settle and hugged her arms together to keep from trembling. She realized now how wrong what she'd done must seem. If only Paul had liked her enough not to tell . . .

"Bernadette, this is a serious matter and must have consequence," David warned.

"David," Hester pleaded.

"Now, Hester, don't interfere. Paul has wanted to be rid of the shoe stitching for less womanly work. Bernadette, you will stitch two pairs of shoes a day, the pair Paul sewed and one more besides. The shoes are to be put by the fireplace where I can inspect them each morning."

"Two pairs?" Hester exclaimed. "You know Paul couldn't get two pairs done in a day."

David ignored Hester. "Do you understand, my girl?"

A mighty rebellion welled up in Bernadette. It propelled her off the bench to face David. "Yes, sir. I understand about the shoes. But I don't think it's fair. Any more than I think it's fair Pardon Crandall is forbidden to visit his daughter or take food to her. It's wrong for the doctor and greengrocer — yes, and the church — to make life so hard for the teacher. I'm not ashamed of trying to take food to her."

"Stolen food," David reminded, his face flushing at her temerity. "And did you speak up so saucy to my brother?"

"No, sir. I never needed to."

"Nor need you to me, nor will you again. And why such softness toward a school you won't go to yourself?"

"I'm not proud of myself to be so afraid to go to a strange

black place like that. And sometimes I ask myself, why not? After all, it's a girls' school and I could learn what I need to there."

"Well," David declared with finality, "no matter what you feel for the school and its niggers, the Bible says, 'Thou shalt not steal.' I suggest you pray on that. In this family we expect everyone to behave as they should. And they do."

"If they do . . ." Bernadette began heatedly, then shut her mouth. Hester's worried face had suddenly stoppered her up. Sore tempted as her anger made her, she couldn't wound Hester worse by tattling on Paul.

With a firm glance down at her and an authoritative nod to his wife, David marched out of the kitchen.

Bernadette sat down on the bench with a thud; she felt like a bellows with all the air pumped out of it.

Hester put an arm around her shoulders. "Bernadette, I've misled you. I'm sorry. I've not misled you about the black school but I've wronged you in letting you think you're free to make choices like taking food there. As a girl you're subject to the dictates of your elders and especially David Fry. As a woman — you must obey a husband." Hester's face worked briefly.

Sitting there, Bernadette felt helplessly pinioned by the bars of a shrinking world. Could she never hope for a freedom all her own? Pulsing within herself was a need to follow her own lead, a violent need to strike out at those who would deny her. Obey! Obey! She'd tried to obey like a soldier ever since she'd got here.

"Dear child, I'll help when I can with the sewing."

"Aunt Hester, will I *ever* get back to Oberlin?" Berna-

101

dette whispered, welcoming comfort this time. "Where will I get the education so I can go back to Oberlin?"

"Yes, where?" The troubled woman turned away in a quandary.

Bernadette loathed shoe sewing. The coarse sandals were shipped from New England for the Southern slaves. Their leather was stiff and thick and toughened her hands as she worked. The needle, filled with awkward thong, squeaked and grunted through the heavy material. Worst of all, nothing of beauty resulted once a pair was finished. All there was to show for the work were the four pennies a pair the store paid David Fry.

Pulling the heavy needle with her teeth, straightening the curled leather with stiff fingers, she was sewing impatiently when Paul came in. He sat down on the settle and began to flip the pages of one of his school books. She knew he wasn't reading.

"I guess you didn't tell on me about shinnying down the tree."

"No," she answered briefly, hoping he'd leave.

"Why not?" Paul asked. His blue eyes challenged her over his book.

"I figured it would upset your ma. Besides, I don't tattle."

There was a considering silence. "Well, I'm beholden to you," Paul spoke reluctantly. "In your place, I'd have tattled. Pa'd lick me if you had told because Ingo and the boys and I crawl in the cider mill. I'm going to give it up."

"That's good."

He got up, stretched elaborately, yawned, and kept his eyes

uneasily away from the shoe in her hand. "Most girls would have got even by tattling."

"I never tattled on Jonathan Fry," Bernadette said.

"Didn't you though?" Paul asked in astonishment. "Did Cousin Jonathan do a lot of bad things?"

"A few things at school . . ."

"Oh," Paul answered, disappointed. "By the way, what are you going to do about school? Forget it? That's what I'd be glad to do."

"Not on your life!" she shot back. "I've been sitting here planning. If your ma and pa consent, I'm going back to common school. I'll study ahead myself, memorize everything. Maybe there'll be a teacher who'll help me, lend me a book or two."

"Sounds foolish to me," Paul replied without much interest. "Though some might call it gritty."

Soon Paul went out carelessly, leaving his school book on the bench beside her.

She laid down the shoe and curiously picked up the book. It was about the Romans and Hannibal. She read eagerly, unmindful of Paul's returning steps. Suddenly his hand reached down and took the book away. "I'd best take it before it's lost."

"I was just reading the part where Hannibal tied burning faggots to his oxen's horns and marched them through the pass to surprise the Romans. What happened to Hannibal?"

"A girl don't need to know about Hannibal," Paul informed her offhandedly. "It's men do the general-ing." He banged out the kitchen door.

She sat and looked at the fire, and would have hated Paul

—but she was sick of hating him. Besides, she guessed, he couldn't possibly realize how much she wanted to know what was in his school book. How could he, when he himself never seemed to want to know about anything except farming and rowdying?

She picked up the shoe.

I'll find out what happened to Hannibal, she vowed. Maybe not in Canterbury, but at Oberlin . . .

Oberlin. There were getting to be a lot of things she needed to find out there.

chapter 12

🌲🌲🌲🌲🌲🌲🌲🌲

S HE HURRIED up the slope in the afternoon sunshine. Paul had seen her head out for North Hill but she wasn't worried. Once he'd realized she hadn't told on him, a mysterious change had brewed in Paul — he would study her sidewise as though enough aware of her at last to try to figure her out. Awkward and wordless, last night he had joined her when she played with Rachel. "My, but you make her crow!" he had remarked admiringly.

July was certainly a hot time to climb hills. Her petticoats stuck to her.

Bernadette spied what she was hunting sitting on a boulder under a tree, sunbonnet in profile, her knees hugged under her chin. Miriam Hosking was gazing down the mountain in the direction of Rhode Island forty miles away.

Bernadette scrambled up beside her, said, "Ouch!" and scooted over to the grass. "It's hot enough to fry an egg on that rock. How do you sit there?"

"Hello," Miriam responded, turning her head; her eyes twinkled. "I'm sitting where it's shady. If I'd known for sure you were coming I'd have spread my skirts and kept two spots cool."

"Mr. Fry took Aunt Hester over to Shaw's farm. I have to be back soon to wash crocks. Was the road clear all the way?"

"I came in the underbrush," Miriam answered, her eyes clouding.

"Nobody at the school saw you leave?"

"No. They're too upset over Miss Crandall's trial. Everyone's thinking just of it."

"What really happened yesterday in Brooklyn?"

"Miss Crandall was let off till December when a new jury's to be assembled in County Court. Judge Eaton dismissed yesterday's jury because it went out and came back three times without agreeing."

"Aunt Hester says the teacher admitted breaking the new Connecticut black laws."

"There's more to it than that." Miriam frowned. "Miss Crandall's lawyers say the black laws are unconstitutional, that the Declaration of Independence gives us freed Negroes the rights of citizens. But Mr. Judson argues the Constitution says persons of color aren't citizens and never can be."

"Oh, dear, it's very complicated." Bernadette sighed, chewing a tall grass stem.

"I don't think so," Miriam disagreed. "I feel like a citizen just as much as I feel like a person. But mainly what everybody's so upset about is that the trial yesterday wasn't fair because Judge Eaton told the jury the new black laws *were* constitutional. That really made Miss Crandall's lawyers angry because a judge hasn't got the right to tell a jury his opinion is fact."

The girls sat in silence for a while.

"Even if she's breaking the law, she'll keep on at her school, won't she?"

"Miss Crandall? Yes."

They watched how the soft clouds were born down in the

sky's womb over Rhode Island. A thought flowed into Bernadette's mind: They were friends. It was as simple as that. Their very silence felt comfortable.

"Miriam . . ."

"Ummm." Miriam sounded sleepy and far away, at ease in the sunshade.

"You told me about your grandmother — Beeljie, you called her. I've thought a lot about her. Do you realize you know more about your grandmother than I do about mine? Mine's dead."

Miriam lay back on the rock. "Grandma Beeljie's certainly not dead," she replied, her tone amused, untesty. "She's always telling about Timbo and what it was like living there when she was a girl."

"Well, what *was* it like?"

"Ummm. Let me see. The city of Timbo was circled by huge African mountains and the air was bright. Close by there were big plantations that grew rice and sweet potatoes and things like peppers and cassavas. The Foulah farmers kept flocks of chickens, goats, sheep, and oxen. Timbo had a double wall of pointed posts on the outside and fire-hardened spear-headed staves on the inside. It had gates with zigzags and loopholes . . ."

"Miss Crandall could use a fence like that!" Bernadette half laughed.

"Well, it'd have to be high enough so's you couldn't throw rotten eggs over it," Miriam reminded.

"Go on."

"Inside Timbo there were wide streets and big houses, but a lot of little houses, too, with paper charms hung on them to ward off thieves and witches. The palace was adobe with a

107

big porch. The king, Beeljie's father, was a Mussulman and knew the Koran. He wore a high headdress and long white robes. Beeljie said her father sat on sheepskin mats while female slaves fanned his feet."

"Slaves!" Bernadette exclaimed. "But I thought Africans . . ." she floundered.

"Africans keep slaves," Miriam explained coolly. "Foulahs often made slaves of other Africans. They even helped round them up to take them to the white traders on the coast. There's no money in Africa; slavery's money instead. Among Foulahs nearly the only punishment for law-breaking was slavery."

"But why would people do that to their own?" Bernadette asked, aghast.

"Why will Dr. Harris not treat Miss Crandall when she's sick or Captain Fenner not sell her food?"

"Yes, but . . ."

"Well, do you want to hear about Grandmother or not?" The old impatience returned to Miriam's voice.

"Tell me about Beeljie," Bernadette agreed. They were getting on too well to risk an argument.

"Grandmother was promised by her father, the Ali, to an old man who was cruel to his wives. Grandmother said she wouldn't marry such a man. So they threw her into Timbo's prison. Since the kin of kings were never killed, it was decided Beeljie would be sold into slavery. When the coffle of slaves set out for the coast, Grandma refused to walk and had to be tied on a litter. Finally to save the other slaves, she walked. But lots of times she tried to dash her head against rocks by the path. She swore they'd never bring her to the ocean."

There was a silence. A meadowlark swooped through the air, trilling.

"But naked, except for a rope around her neck, Princess Beeljie was brought to the ocean after all. Her father, the Ali, said to sell her for her weight in fat. That was the most insulting thing he could have asked, something cattle were measured in. But the white trader took pity, and after examining her, he bought her for a tub of salt. Anyway, with hundreds of others she was locked in the barracoon, the slave pen on the beach. Two days before they loaded the boat, her head was shaved and she was branded."

"Oh no!" Bernadette shuddered.

"Well," Miriam added, "it was a small iron and it was heated only enough so as to blister but not burn. Still, I guess I don't feel like telling about the ocean trip, not now anyway."

"You know about the ocean trip?"

"Yes. Grandmother's told us everything."

"Do you look like your grandmother, Miriam?"

Miriam swerved around on her stone. She stared with defiance at Bernadette. "No," she declared. "In looks I favor the Coromantees. Grandmother Beeljie isn't brown like me, she's bronze. The Foulahs look more like Moors. My mother says when my grandmother Beeljie was younger, she was beautiful and carried herself like a princess-born. I'm not beautiful."

Large-eyed, Bernadette studied Miriam's face. "Aren't you?" she asked simply.

Suddenly Miriam threw her head back and laughed merrily. "No," she finally gasped. "No, I'm not beautiful. Even black folks don't think I am."

"Well," Bernadette answered sympathetically, "I'm not beautiful, either. I'm too skinny and my face is plain. But I don't care. There's too much else to worry about."

"You have maple-sugar eyes," Miriam chuckled, "and the friendliest smile. And your hair is shiny and has red in it. Red hair means you have lots of gumption. What do you worry about?"

"What do I worry about? Right now how many crocks I have to scald. Sometimes I see crocks in my sleep . . ."

They both smiled. Neither was a stranger to hard work. "No, but what do you *really* worry about?" Miriam pressed.

So Bernadette sat under the tree and told her friend about Ohio, about Pastor and Jonathan Fry, about Oberlin, about not being able to go to school in Canterbury but needing to go because it was the only way back to Oberlin.

Finally they talked lazily about lots of things — Rachel's new baby tricks, how many slave shoes Bernadette had sewn, the fun of climbing in the filled hay mows, of a new black student who, in learning to braid her hair, had by mistake braided herself to the bedpost.

A distant cowbell, mellow and peaceful, reminded them time had run out.

"Next Wednesday?"

"Next Wednesday," Bernadette promised, jumping off her rock. "Watch out for the road."

"Don't break any crocks . . ." All the way down the hill Miriam answered Bernadette's wave.

She bit the end of the quill and dipped it in the ink box.

"Dear Pastor, Mrs. Fry, Jonathan, Ruth, Naomi, Seth, Willy, and Anna," she began. Before she could checkrein herself she was pouring out the whole story of Miss Crandall's seminary and the strange things told to her by her new friend Miriam. At the end of the letter she put the question she'd promised herself she wouldn't ask.

Pastor, how would you feel about a single white girl going to school with all blacks? I'm not really planning it, but I just wondered.

chapter 13

⅋⅋⅋⅋⅋⅋⅋⅋

Pₐᵤₗ ₗₑₐₙₑₔ into the Lewises's barn door and whistled softly. Out of the dark came an answering whistle. "Hssst! Over here. Set a spell and have a smoke."

Guided by the round red glow of a homemade cigar, Paul found Ingo in an empty horse stall. Paul sat down in the straw, reached for the cigar, and puffed deeply. He coughed so hard he nearly dropped it. He passed it back to Ingo.

"Where's the other boys?"

"I reckon they're not coming tonight. You get away without that girl seeing?"

"Yes."

"Has she tol' yet?"

"No. And I don't think she's going to. She says she won't."

"Don't you believe a girl!" Ingo advised Paul loftily. "I wouldn't believe a girl if my life depended on it."

"I don't know," Paul answered; something made him shuffle uneasily in the stall. "Bernadette's not so bad. She works awful hard for Ma; works cheerful, too. And she does love my little sister — totes her all the time."

"Girls always work hard and love babies," Ingo retorted.

"Your sister Cindy don't," Paul reminded. Cindy Lewis was lazy as sin, lounging barefoot around the kitchen in a ragged apron. And Paul had never once seen Cindy lift the

113

Lewis baby out of the cradle, even when his squawks were deafening.

"Oh, well, Cindy . . ." Ingo snorted as though Cindy were beneath argument. "Look how this Bernadette wants to go to school. Any girl that crazy to shut herself up in a school — well, you could never depend on someone like that."

"No, I suppose not," Paul agreed. But inside he was churned up. His feelings about Bernadette — once crystal-clear resentment of her as an intruder in his family — grew more muddled daily.

"She go to North Hill to meet that nigger?"

"Yes. I was out with Shep bringing the milk cows in when she came home from that way."

"See, I told you! Another crazy thing! Why would she want to meet a nigger?"

"I don't know, Ingo. Lonely, maybe . . ."

"Lonely!" Ingo exclaimed disbelievingly, his cigar butt arching through the dark. "Lonely for a nigger? I don't see how you stand for it, Paul! She brings that black crow to your house and then makes you tote her into the school, all fainted . . ."

"She'd not have been at my house or fainted, either one, if you hadn't stoned her."

There was a hot, steamy silence. "Well, I'm glad I did," Ingo replied defensively. "And I didn't get thrashed for it either, when your ma complained to my pa. My pa said it was just what the black wench had coming to her."

"Stoning's mean. She was all purple under her eyes and on her cheeks."

"Well, isn't that a pity!" Ingo exclaimed sarcastically. He

stood up so that the cigar shone like a fiery cinder above Paul's head. "What's come over you? You getting soft?"

"No, I'm not!"

"Well then, quit talking mush."

It *was* mush, Paul concluded. A few weeks ago he'd never have thought a thing about Bernadette's doing his shoe sewing, let alone about the black girl's purple cheek. Savagely he tried to snuff out these strange stirrings in himself. He'd told himself to come into town tonight to have some fun, fun like they'd always had.

"Why don't we go to North Hill someday, spy on the girls on the rocks?" Ingo suggested.

"What fun would there be in that?" Paul questioned promptly. "I'd rather do something at the school."

Ingo finally answered. "Yeah, I been thinking about the school a lot. Say, you know what I figured when I was cleaning the horse stalls?"

Paul let out his breath softly; the knots in his stomach eased. "No. What'd you figure, Ingo?"

"What would they do for water if we fouled their well?"

So long as it didn't have anything more to do with Bernadette, Paul supposed in those first moments of relief he would have agreed to anything. "Ingo, that'd be a great idea."

"Neighbors won't lend them water. Old Pardon lives too far away. Oh, they could put out a hogshead for rainwater but we've had a hot dry spell and no letup's coming. Why, we might just do what that stupid hung jury over to Brooklyn with their three times disagreeing didn't succeed in doing."

"Then maybe the Supreme Court at Hartford won't even

have to make a new decision," Paul rejoined. But the knots came back in his stomach. Fouling a well was a far cry from rotten-egg throwing and cabbage smashing.

"Let's get a move on, then," Ingo said. "I got a bucket and you can carry a keg. C'mon. Wish the rest of the fellows was here."

Paul wished they were, too. Then maybe in all the excitement, the dark and all, he could sneak away. Suddenly, deep down, he wanted to do that. But he and Ingo were alone; no help for it but to run with Ingo . . .

They hid in the bushes of the school's backyard. Except for a frog's croak, there wasn't another sound.

When they had decided the coast was clear, they crept up to the black bulky house, found the well lid, and untied it. The contents of the bucket and keg plopped into the cool clear water.

They ran back, shoveled again with arms aching, then returned to the school. While they waited in the deep shadow of the back shed, Ingo said he wished they could find a window to pry up in the house because without good water the niggers weren't going to be in Canterbury much longer; then the fun would be over . . .

They dropped the second load of manure in the well, ran along the house's foundation toward the road, and stooped by one of the basement windows. Ingo grunted as he tried to pull it up. Paul tried the second and third windows.

"Won't come," Paul breathed, not really trying. "Let's get out of here!"

"Them sills is dry and splintery," Ingo observed.

Finally they both ran so hard neither had breath to say more.

116

Paul trudged into his own yard. He hoped he had the wind to get up the tree to his window. He came to the great tamarack, raised his hands to spit on them. He was thinking, *Whoo! My hands smell!* when he got the worst scare of his born days.

She was a little thing; she skipped and skimmed across the lawn, a darker shadow sailing right out of the tree-shadowed night at him.

"I thought you said you weren't going to town anymore," Bernadette hissed.

Paul's teeth nearly jarred loose, he stopped so short. "W-what are you doing out here?"

"A weasel got in the hen house. The chickens made a terrible commotion; two are dead. Your pa just went upstairs. If you're smart you'll wait a minute before you climb that tree."

"Did Pa come looking for me?" Paul breathed.

"No. I said you'd had a stomachache when you went to bed. Your ma said to let you sleep, then. So I helped your pa."

"You helped Pa," he murmured. His head wagged. "I be in your debt, Bernadette." He, Paul Fry, saying it humble-like! Paul Fry wanting to reach out gratefully for this slim girl's hand lost in the dark somewhere!

He must have stepped too close, because suddenly she said, "What's that smell? It's you . . . You smell funny. You smell *awful!*"

"Yes . . . well, I . . ." He couldn't think fast like her. Then it burst out of him: "I wish I didn't smell awful; I'm not proud of smelling this way."

"Oh, Paul," Bernadette said wearily, as though she'd given

117

up expecting him to make any sense. "Climb up the tree and get to bed!"

The triumphant town declared it was fatal for such a large establishment to be without fresh water. Bernadette was stunned by the news, wondered if such a fiendishly simple act could bring about the school's downfall.

Hester shook her head in dismay; David's silence was judgmental. Bernadette's feelings — after shock — swung like a pendulum between her own school interests and Miriam and Miss Crandall, both growing vividly real to her.

Another thing she puzzled about: Paul had said he went at night to the cider mill. Under the tree it hadn't been cider she smelled on him, she was pretty sure. A terrible seed of suspicion was planted in her about Paul. But something that serious . . . she'd wait and see.

Bernadette and the town soon learned what it was to reckon with the spirit of a Crandall.

In defiance of the law, every morning and evening Pardon Crandall — set faced and thinly erect — drove his farm wagon in and out of town carrying full water kegs to his daughter and bringing back empty ones.

chapter 14

✟✟✟✟✟✟✟✟

Bernadette finished her seventeenth pair of sandals and lined them up carefully by the hearth. She wandered out to the kitchen steps to sit by herself and think. In her pocket she carried a well-worn letter from Pastor Fry, and it was this letter she couldn't keep out of her mind.

In part it read:

> . . . you wonder what I think of your asking to go to the Negro girls' seminary — I'm opposed to your attendance there — While some of us are beginning to deplore slavery and wish to abolish it, that doesn't mean we urge fraternity with blacks, Bernadette — It is well known the moral state of the free black is low and I should not like you to live among them.

> At her age Hester is slow to recover from the birth of Rachel and needs you, so you must be patient while all of us try to work out a suitable school plan.

> Be encouraged that Brother David Fry tells me it's the solemn expectation of the villagers Miss Crandall's black school will soon be a thing of the past and she will return to instructing the white girls she was brought to Canterbury to teach — Then your troubles will be over . . .

Bernadette was stuffing the letter back in her apron pocket when a man on horseback rode into the farmyard. She saw that it was the local Negro agent for William Lloyd Garrison's newspaper, *The Liberator*. David had been badgering Hester about *The Liberator* lately. She watched apprehensively as the young black man dismounted. She greeted him, put her head in the kitchen door to tell David who called, then went back to sit down on the step.

David appeared and said briskly, "Good evening."

"I've brought the newspaper." The man held it out. He pointed proudly to black headlines which announced SAVAGE BARBARITY! MISS CRANDALL IMPRISONED!

"No, we'll not buy it anymore," David replied, waving it away. "I never approved *The Liberator* coming to our house in the first place."

"But it tells all about Miss Crandall," the agent protested.

"Indeed it does. And is responsible for making a martyr of her. I've told my wife I'll not have it on the premises."

"But all over the country, people are beginning to know about her."

"More's the pity. Good day, sir." He slammed the door. "Good day."

With downcast eyes, Bernadette watched the boots beside her turn and start down the steps. Then she dared to look up into the agent's brown face, somber with disappointment. Suddenly she longed to say something to him which would restore his smile. But she couldn't think of anything.

The newspaper agent started toward his tethered horse; then, while she watched, he turned back. As he walked toward her he drew from his coverall a wrapped bundle.

"Excuse me, daughter. Are you Miss Bernadette?"

Startled, she answered simply, "Yes."

"I've brought you something," he told her, almost smiling. Filled with wonder, Bernadette took the small packet he held out. She mumbled her thanks, jumped off the stoop, and ran to the nearby quiet of the woodshed. Whatever it was, something warned her it should be opened privately.

She bit the twine knot and pulled it loose. Pages of *The Liberator* wrapped three small, dark books. Bernadette stooped over them to see what the lettering on the fronts read.

Colburn's *First Lessons*
Adams's *New Arithmetic*
Watts's *On The Mind*

Her hand shook. She pulled a torn piece of paper out of the last volume and read the large, unformed writing:

"I'm sorry I can't find what happened to Hannibal in here. Miriam."

Bernadette knew she held in her hands the most precious things Miriam owned — Miriam's hard-won books, generously lent to her.

From the tumble of new-chopped wood on which she sat, she looked unseeingly at the familiar gnarled maple lengths stacked to the roof line, the hogshead of drying brown kindling needles called diddle-dees, Paul's ax wedged into the big log, heady-smelling green pine needles strewn thick on the earthen floor.

She didn't see because she was feeling so much. She rubbed her finger on the book covers as though they might come to life, make clear to her what was hidden.

121

Even though Miriam had invited friendship, to befriend Miriam hadn't been easy. Miriam had built a wall around herself. But Bernadette had taken that invitation and breached that wall. And was fervently glad of it.

Tears in her eyes, Bernadette's hopes flowed back strongly — no longer the delicate hopes of an enthusiastic child but more durable, determined hopes, hopes beyond fantasy.

From the evening light which streamed in the door, Bernadette turned to the first page of Watts's *On The Mind*. She tried to read. But she couldn't read for thinking of Miriam. Miriam! She who — as Pastor Fry claimed — was of low moral estate.

For the first time, Bernadette doubted Pastor Fry. She felt a last childish dependence dissolve. In life she must believe or disbelieve in her own way.

chapter 15

✝✝✝✝✝✝✝✝✝

David took his place at the head of the supper table.

Bernadette and Paul made short work of the eating, since Rachel fussed in her cradle for attention and Paul had chores to do.

The husband and wife supped quietly, paying no attention to Rachel's chuckling as she lay in Bernadette's lap, nor to the calf's bawling from the barn, or a dog's howl from the distant woods.

"I'd like to go this Sabbath to the Quaker meeting at Black Hill," Bernadette heard Hester say. It was the strained tone which caught her ear. "The Quakers are inviting the girls of Prudence Crandall's school to come there for service, since the Canterbury church locks them out."

"And not go to church with me?" David asked incredulously.

"I can't go there any longer, David. What our church has done against the black school I can never forgive."

"But it's the church of your birth, Hester. It's the church of my birth."

"I'm not asking *you* to go to the Quakers, David; I'm only asking that you let me go."

There was an awful silence; Rachel's coo sounded like a shout.

"I'll walk across the fields with Bernadette, who can help

carry Rachel." There was desperation in that voice, touching in its pleading dignity; there was love in that voice and pain at making David Fry unhappy.

"But you'd be going one place and I another!"

"Only till the school matter resolves itself, David. I want to stand with Prudence Crandall. I can't worship with her enemies."

"You would stand with Prudence Crandall against your husband? Your husband is your enemy?"

"You know you're not, David."

Bernadette dared to look up from the baby; the husband and wife leaned tensely over their plates. She lifted Rachel to her shoulder and held her there, careful not to look again.

"Say no more, Hester," David finally advised harshly. "You'll come to church with me and do your duty as you should."

"My duty is to attend Black Hill, and that is where I must go, with or without your permission," Hester answered him. "The Good Book is wrong to say man is the master of woman; God is. And God has spoken to me and told me the things that are done against that school are wrong. Would I had told you so when you punished Bernadette, but I was not yet as sure of my conscience as I am now since you cut off *The Liberator*'s coming."

"Hester . . ." David began, outrage choking him.

But she got up and went stiffly from the kitchen looking neither to right nor left.

Bernadette realized David was suddenly conscious of her sitting there. From his face, Bernadette sensed she had just witnessed one of the most upsetting events in all the Frys' married days.

David pushed his plate away as though its food disgusted him. He went to the mantel, got his pipe, tamped tobacco in it, and went to the door. She knew he was struggling for calm.

"Would you go to Black Hill with Mrs. Fry?" he asked in a harsh voice.

"Yes, sir."

"Because she asked or because you believe as she does?"

"Both," she replied.

"And if I forbade you?"

"I don't know," Bernadette whispered, hugging Rachel.

"Well, it's not a fair question to ask, not fair to put you in the center of our muddle." David sighed. He continued to lean on the doorjamb. Smoke billowed over his shoulder; he made sucking sounds which should have been from contentment. "You know, Bernadette, a husband has rights. He can beat his wife, proper and legal, in Connecticut state."

"Oh, no, sir . . ."

David turned, fixed her with a steady eye. "I never would, of course; I tremble at the thought. But I *do* have that right."

"Yes, sir."

"And other rights, too. All Mrs. Fry's property became mine when I married her. If God sent misfortune to us and Mrs. Fry had to work — do laundering, for example — every penny she earned would be mine."

"I pray there won't be such a misfortune."

"There won't be," David promised. "I'd never let my wife wash another man's shirts for the coin. But do you know, if I die, making no other provision, Hester could stay in this house only forty days? Yes, the law says it . . ."

125

"Surely it would never be that way between you and Aunt Hester."

"It would not. I married the proudest girl in the township, loved her then, and love her now. I'm merely recounting my husband's rights. I need to consider them in order to come to my decision and also for your instructing. If I die, Bernadette, I could will Rachel away from Hester to anyone I wished . . . to my brother in Ohio, to you even —"

"Oh, sir, I should want Rachel terribly but not at the expense of taking her away from her mother."

A grim smile hovered around David's lips. "Rachel would stay with her mother, have no fear of that."

He came over to the hearth, put his foot up on the settle, looked down at Bernadette, then at Rachel asleep with her head drooped over the girl's shoulder, one limp arm dangling.

"I wish Hester had never heard the word 'abolition.' I wish Miss Crandall had stayed over at Plainfield and never blighted Canterbury. Because of both, troubles have come between me and my wife — except for the loss of our children, the first serious trouble we've ever had."

"I'm sorry, sir."

Curiously, David picked up the soft helpless fist of his baby daughter. "Well," he concluded, "there's nothing for it but to let Mrs. Fry do this mad thing. God has told her to walk to Black Hill with you and the baby. Somehow I'll make her excuses to the pastor at church. But if Hester goes to the Quakers, she goes without my consent. No word of permission will ever pass my lips."

"Yes, sir," Bernadette answered. Despite her disagreement with him and sympathy for Hester, she felt sorry for him —

regretful at troubles which must seem to both like sand in an oyster which brought no pearl, nettles in a smooth stand of grain, a fleshy canker which was beginning to hurt when touched.

chapter 16

🌲🌲🌲🌲🌲🌲🌲🌲🌲

Hester never glanced back as Paul and David rocked down the lane in the buggy. But Bernadette couldn't help looking. David sat with the reins held high, his ramrod back disapproving, while Paul stared around in bewilderment at his mother's shawled back.

"Come, Bernadette, it's a long way to Black Hill," Hester reminded.

A long walk it was, with the precious baby passed from one to the other to ease their weariness. They climbed Neighbor Shaw's stone fences. They cut through crackling hot, suffocating Indian-corn fields which closed them in, then stumbled over ripening pumpkins with huge, entangling vines. But at last they panted up the country road to the meetinghouse sitting high on Black Hill. Early September sun shone on the plain little building nestled in a yellowing grove of maple trees. Horses and wagons were pulled up beside it.

Bernadette tried to stamp the dust from her shoes, but for once Hester allowed no time for tidying.

"We enter this way." She nodded to Bernadette, going up to a door as though she'd been born a member of the sect.

Once inside, Bernadette saw why it was important to enter correctly. They settled down on the side where only females sat — a group of dark-dressed, white-capped females, old and young. Across the center aisle sat the men and boys, hatted even in church in broad, flat-brimmed black hats.

Bernadette's first inquiring glance was for Miss Crandall's girls. Rows of straw bonnets stood out among white-winged caps. Bernadette, relieved to find Miriam's blue flowers, next studied the meetinghouse itself.

If it were any plainer it would be like a barn, she thought. The large rustic room had no altar, no pulpit — nothing but rows of simple wood seats. At the head of the congregation the benches were turned around, and on these a score of dignified country folk faced the rest. Surely she wouldn't have to stare into those faces all morning! Bernadette ducked her head hurriedly.

She listened to the sounds around her, the creaking of a bench, a child scratching, a foot scraping. Windows were open and a horse stomped and whinnied. But nothing was being said, sung, read, or even recited. Apparently there was no pastor or priest to lead them, or if there were, he was very late.

Bewildered, Bernadette untied Rachel's bonnet, automatically licked her finger, and rubbed the fine dark hair upward from the nape of the baby's neck. She was trying to make Rachel's hair curl although Hester disapproved of such vanity and even now shook her head at Bernadette.

But what must I do with my thoughts? Bernadette wondered in panic.

The silence deepened; Bernadette could hear it grow. Even among the young, rustling gradually hushed.

Rachel squirmed; Hester took her. Bernadette clasped her hands together, found them unpleasantly damp, and laid them carefully apart in her lap. She counted the warp and the woof threads in the material of her skirt. She thought of her sins — she had ever so many of them. But her disobedient mind kept slipping away from such unpleasantness.

After what seemed like an eon of time, an old man rose and, laying aside his broad hat, quavered, "But Thou, O Lord, art a god full of compassion, and gracious, long-suffering, and plenteous in mercy and truth."

He sat down. The silence was now most profound.

Bernadette stopped counting threads. That first Sabbath in Canterbury, the minister had shrilled that the Lord had cursed Canaan.

How glad she was the black girls could hear in this meetinghouse not curses, but love instead. The silence which had closed her out and left her anxiously by herself, crept out to her, hovered magically near, finally enfolded her with the others. Her body relaxed. She shut her eyes and rested in the stillness of her own soul, but rested somehow neither alone nor far from God.

Another Quaker, rising to speak, said: "Shew me a token for good; that they which hate me may see it, and be ashamed, because thou, Lord, has helpen me, and comforted me . . ."

Even a woman spoke, which at first startled, then pleased Bernadette. No pastor ever appeared, nor was there singing or kneeling.

Bernadette was surprised when a mysterious stirring presaged the breakup of the service. The old woman beside her reached over and shook her hand; Hester was greeted on the other side. Rachel opened a sleepy blue eye.

While Hester talked with several women, Bernadette

eagerly followed the black girls out into the meeting yard.

"Will you attend here?" were Miriam's first words.

"Mrs. Fry would like to come here every Sunday. She says she can't go anymore to the church in Canterbury because of the unchristian folk there."

"There are some unchristian folk here, too," Miriam added drily, "but also many true Quakers. Miss Crandall tells us the Quakers have had a great quarrel and have dropped away from leading against slavery as they once did."

"I don't know anything about them," Bernadette confessed. "They have plain ways but comforting, too."

Still, Quaker Meeting wasn't what she wanted to talk to Miriam about. Bernadette reached for the black girl's hand. Miriam let herself be touched, then as though forgiving something, returned the gesture. Friends, yes, but a distance to travel together before friends wholly . . .

"Thank you for the books, Miriam. I'll never be able to tell you how grateful I am."

Miriam's face took on a dusky discomfort. It stayed that way for a second, then laughter lit it, faintly derisive. Bernadette sensed then it was sometimes easier for Miriam to feel scorned than feel loved, easier to be rebuked than thanked.

But finally Miriam's eyes warmed. "I wanted you to have them. You want to go to school so much. Will you be at North Hill next week?"

Just as Bernadette was promising to be at North Hill, Prudence Crandall bustled up. Hester Fry was with her. Bernadette was overjoyed the two women had spoken together at last. But Miss Crandall wore a busy, preoccupied air.

"Hester Fry, we are planning a gala at the school this fall,

131

soon. You and Bernadette are cordially invited to attend the exercises which will be on a Saturday."

"Oh, could you?" Miriam asked Bernadette eagerly.

Bernadette looked to Hester and instantly read her thoughts. To be away on a Saturday from the farm? Be away for a purpose no one would approve? After the struggle of even getting to this meeting?

"We'd both like to," Hester answered slowly, "but for me it wouldn't be possible. Still, perhaps Bernadette can attend."

"She'd be most welcome to hear our girls recite. A few other friends will join us. Come, Miriam," Miss Crandall commanded, and hurried away toward the wagons.

Already one wagon was filled to overflowing with small Negro girls who lined the side benches. Bernadette watched the teacher climb with quick energy to the front seat beside her father. Miriam fell in with the older girls, who got in with young Reuben Crandall. Miriam turned and raised her hand to Bernadette. "North Hill," her bright eyes signaled. The wagons rumbled out of the yard and onto the road.

Hester and Bernadette climbed the hill. When they got to the top, far below they could see the wagons and horses winding along the dirt road, the second wagon hanging back to avoid the dust. Meetinghouse chaises and horses followed, traveling sedately.

Rachel's hungry fret turned to an earnest cry. The mother sought a shady place. The trees on the hills and in the valleys were turning citron and gold, scarlet and copper-tinged. Bernadette leaned on a tree trunk and musingly watched the Negro wagons till they rolled out of sight around a bend.

"She must be very tired and very worried," Hester observed.

"The teacher?"

"Yes. As for the exercises at the school, Bernadette, I want you to attend. You like Miriam, don't you?"

"I like her now. At first I was afraid of her. But when I saw her stoned something changed inside me, I don't know just what. But I'm scared for Miriam — she does things the others don't dare."

"So I suspect. She's also generous with her scorn."

"Still, she can be a very good friend," Bernadette answered quietly.

"That too," Hester agreed, and said no more.

Hester buttoned her basque and got reluctantly to her feet. "How beautiful fall is," she said with a sigh.

Paul met them in the orchard, his eyes curious. "Pastor asked for you at church," he remarked pointedly to his mother. "Pa told him you'd soon come back to service."

"It was kind of Pastor to inquire for me," Hester answered serenely.

"Won't you be coming to church, Mother? You won't be going to the Quakers always, will you?"

"In the wintertime we can't walk there," Hester reminded her son sensibly. "Still, even in winter I don't intend to go to our church. Not all the church people are savage but those who are its main pillars seem to be. Meanwhile, Bernadette and I will have two months at Black Hill, at least. I met the teacher today. I believe we liked one another . . . Perhaps we'll try to start a female antislave society. There are beginning to be such societies — Miss Crandall told me."

"And how did *you* like the Quakers?" Paul asked Bernadette, catching up with her.

She was tired and heated from carrying Rachel; she answered more shortly than she meant to. She liked them, she said, but no more.

Stung, Paul dropped back. So Bernadette was being hoity-toity! Well, he'd leave them both alone. Still, seeing them together like that — bound by some strange pact — raised a new resentment in Paul. If Bernadette weren't here, his mother couldn't go to Black Hill alone, what with toting the baby and all. And if his ma kept on toting the baby to the Quakers, pretty soon it'd be all over the village his ma had turned odd and joined the Quakers.

After the well-fouling Paul had shied away from Ingo Lewis for a spell. But now he couldn't wait to hightail into town and complain to him.

chapter 17

✝✝✝✝✝✝✝✝✝

Y OU'VE FINISHED the heavy part, child, now run on. Go to North Hill, Bernadette." Hester smiled through the thin smoke haze.

Bernadette poured the last of the sweet cider and peeled apples into the bubbly, fragrant brown butter. Hester dipped her stirring paddle into the huge kettle which hung over the backyard fire.

Bernadette didn't even stop to change her sticky apron. As she ran on the ridge trail she figured she'd be a sight by North Hill with dust stuck to her apple-buttery face and messy dress. She crested the spiny hill and paused to notice autumn on the ridges and valleys which rolled down to Rhode Island. How beautiful North Hill would be when September turned to October! But there was sadness in her realization, too. Paul would get to go off to school. Snow would fall, and she and Miriam couldn't meet at North Hill or even at the Quaker meeting.

But at home there would be Rachel, who grew more interesting every day. And when Bernadette wasn't working, there'd be Miriam's books to read and reread, while trying not to wear the pages out as she memorized them.

Strange, but when she got to their meeting place Miriam wasn't on their special rock.

Bernadette's long skirt caught her bare foot as she clambered up the height. *I'd be a worse sight if I lost my two front teeth;* she grinned ruefully, catching herself in time. She sat down, panting.

She pushed back her sunbonnet, wiped her face with her apron, and felt her sticky forehead. Time passed.

Miriam had never been late before. Miriam had always come.

Bernadette lay back, her eyes heavy lidded. Soon they closed.

She woke with a start, sat bolt upright, jumped up, shaded her eyes, and looked in all directions. Maybe Miriam had run into trouble on the turnpike again. Flashing through Bernadette's memory was a picture of Miriam cowering on the road, her arms shielding her head, her skirts a circle of color.

Bernadette paced on the rock. *I wonder, I wonder . . .*

No point just waiting here. I'll go to meet her, she concluded.

Taking advantage of the late summer's low water and to avoid the tollkeeper, Miriam usually forded the river instead of crossing the turnpike bridge. Bernadette was crossing the turnpike to reach Miriam's usual fording spot when the insistent clap of a horse drew her glance down the road.

"Halloo, Bernadette!"

Why, the voice sounded like Paul's! But for a moment Bernadette could recognize neither horse nor rider.

Then as the horse ran pell-mell down upon her, she saw it was Ingo Lewis — with Paul hanging on behind him — both astride an old white mare.

"They've arrested 'em — going to put 'em all in jail in

Brooklyn!" Paul shouted, waving his ragged field hat. Ingo sawed on the reins and the mare crow-hopped to a dusty stop. Paul nearly fell off sideways.

"Yep, going to clear out the kit and caboodle of 'em." Ingo looked down with satisfaction. "We're going to Brooklyn to see the fun."

"You mean Miss Crandall and her girls?"

"Well, of course . . ."

"Paul, could I come with you?" Bernadette pleaded.

"Three on this swayback mare?" Ingo asked incredulously. "She's our old workhorse; she can hardly get up and down the rows as it is."

"You get her going mighty fast, Ingo," Paul remonstrated. "We might as well take Bernadette. It's not too far and she never gets to see anything."

"Well, maybe she should see her friends took off to jail." Ingo grinned. "Hop up behind me if you can find a bone to land on."

Ingo steered the horse to a stump by the road. Paul slid off and helped Bernadette sit astraddle. She hesitated to put her arms around Ingo's waist, then grabbed him tight when Paul startled her by landing behind her with a thud.

She wasn't the only startled one. The old mare took off like a Fourth-of-July barrel had exploded under her. They tore up the turnpike bouncing in dreadful disunity, slipping from side to side.

"Ingo, slow down!" Paul shouted. "She's too big to get my legs around!"

"Don't want to miss anything!" Ingo yelled back. "Just hold tight!"

They splashed through the river — Ingo wouldn't risk his

pa catching him at the toll — climbed the bank, and hit the Brooklyn Road below the village.

"Haven't seen the sheriff's wagon yet," Ingo observed. "Maybe we'll beat them after all." With that he gave the horse a great kick in the flanks, and once more the mare proved her spunk.

She reared like a racehorse. Bernadette clutched Ingo for dear life. But behind her she felt Paul grab wildly, vainly, then disappear.

"Ingo, Paul's bucked off!"

"Hey, Ingo — stop!" There was an indignant cry behind her. She dared look over her shoulder only fleetingly. Paul was standing in the road brushing off the seat of his pantaloons, shouting to beat the band, his face red and his mouth an angry O.

"Ingo, get Paul —"

"Can't stop." Ingo panted. "Hang on!" With that, they jogged around a curve and Paul's clamor grew fainter and fainter. Finally she couldn't hear Paul at all.

"He's going to be mad at you!"

"Don't scare me," Ingo declared. "I could beat him one hand tied behind me."

"I thought he was your friend."

"Well, he is. Only he lives on that high-toned big farm with his high-toned folks."

"I think it's mean to leave him."

"You want to see those wagons empty the niggers at the jail, don't you?"

Of course, she had to see Miriam! "Yes," she agreed reluctantly.

It was a wild ride to Brooklyn. Bernadette thought many

a time she'd land up just as Paul had and knew she'd get left behind, too. But she hung desperately to Ingo and horse, and finally — at last and short of breath — they jogged under the great elms of Brooklyn's village green.

Ingo said he knew where the jail was and headed straight there. But when the old mare, snorting and heaving, delivered them, nothing was tied up at the jail's hitching post.

"We must have beat 'em." Ingo chortled. "Hop off. We'll wait in the shade of the green. That way we can see all the filled wagons rumble up."

They sat uncomfortably under a maple tree. Silently she worried about Miriam. Ingo fidgeted and jumped up every minute to check the village street for wagons.

"Guess it takes a long time to load all them niggers in!"

"They're twenty girls at the school now."

"Yep, and the teacher and the teacher's sister and that young feller."

"Mr. Burleigh," Bernadette supplied. "He teaches, too."

"You know a lot about the school, don't you?"

"Some."

"Guess you find out at Black Hill on Sundays. My pa would drag my ma around the kitchen if she ran off to a different church meeting like that."

"Mr. Fry wouldn't drag Mrs. Fry anywhere," Bernadette answered coldly.

"Well, he oughter," Ingo insisted, his ruddy jaw stuck out.

They must have waited half an hour when down the street bowled the Canterbury sheriff's chaise. Sitting beside him were Eliza Gasko and Miriam Hosking.

"Miriam!" Bernadette gasped. She ran up to the chaise as it rolled to a stop. "Miriam, what's happened?"

"Yeah, where are the other black girls?" Ingo asked.

"Get down, young ladies," the Canterbury sheriff ordered curtly.

Miriam jumped down beside Bernadette. "I've come with Eliza. She's refused to testify to the state's lawyers so she's to lodge in the jail."

"But they said at Fenner's Store *everyone* was arrested," Ingo spoke up in an aggrieved voice.

"Everyone? Not yet, anyway. Just Eliza. But Reverend Kneeland's refused, too, and says he'll go to jail before he'll testify against Miss Crandall. Mary Benson, she's ordered to appear before Attorney Judson. Oh, and Mr. Burleigh, he's going to be coming here, too. He'll testify but only on one fact — that we learn as well as white girls."

"Miriam, will you have to stay in *there?*"

"I expect so," Miriam answered, iron in her voice.

"Come along, young ladies, no more whispering with this pair. Ingo, you skeedaddle home and be quick about it, you hear? And stay out of trouble on the way . . ."

"But, Sheriff," Ingo whined, "I thought all the brushy-haired girls was to be slapped in jail."

"Jail wouldn't have room for them," the sheriff of Canterbury replied shortly.

"Miriam . . ."

"Don't worry . . ."

And those were the last words they could say to each other before Eliza and Miriam were escorted inside.

Bernadette stood and looked up at the county jail. Would they put Miriam in the same wife-murderer's cell they'd put Miss Crandall? If only she could go in with Miriam! By now Bernadette knew how scared Miriam often was, scared underneath most of the time, as Miriam had finally admitted at North Hill. That's why her friend's firm voice didn't fool Bernadette.

"Come on." Ingo pulled Bernadette's sleeve. "It's a long ride home and I suppose I'll get thrashed for swiping the mare. It warn't no fun at all — just the sheriff and a pair. Not worth a thrashing a'tall."

"Seems to me," Bernadette retorted, "they're making trouble for a lot of the school folks. Eliza and Miriam, Reverend Kneeland, Mary Benson, Mr. Burleigh . . ."

"Not trouble enough for enough of them," Master Ingo answered.

As Bernadette clambered up on the horse and gingerly put her arms around Ingo, she felt more like pinching him than resting her arms there peaceably.

In the mellow, late-afternoon sunshine, Miss Crandall's school loomed sedate, dignified, four-square. Ambling past it, Bernadette could imagine a calm and purposeful Prudence Crandall come to the end of a day, lessons finished, supper begun.

It eased her mind, just looking up at the seminary. Folks at Black Hill Meeting said Miss Crandall was growing to be the most prayed-for woman in the United States. Powerful friends — including the very rich reformer, Mr. Tappan — traveled all the way from New York to visit her. Fiery William Lloyd Garrison was still her chief spokesman. In Brooklyn, Reverend Sam May stood staunch. Also in Brooklyn, they were even printing a special newspaper called *The Unionist* in defense of her.

With such support, Miriam and Eliza couldn't stay in jail long.

Bernadette felt a lot better after they'd passed the school. Ingo, apparently, felt worse. "Wish they'd burn the place down," he declared.

chapter 18

✿✿✿✿✿✿✿✿✿

Next Sabbath the ritual continued. Scowling, David drove off with Paul while Hester and Bernadette bundled Rachel in her blankets and set out for the Black Hill Quaker meeting.

Miriam was at Meeting. "Eliza and I were only kept at jail a few hours," she confided to Bernadette. "It hardly amounted to anything . . ."

From all sides adoring dark eyes turned on Miriam and Eliza.

"She wasn't even afraid . . ."

"You weren't, were you, Miriam?"

"No, of course not." Miriam shrugged nonchalantly.

But in the shadow of the wagon, Miriam put her hand in Bernadette's. "I *was* scared," she whispered, "but I don't dare tell *them.*"

On the way to Meeting, Bernadette and Hester were always too hurried to talk. But coming home was different, since from the teacher, they had learned all the current abolition news.

Prudence Crandall reported the South was in an uproar over Britain's West Indian Emancipation Bill, fearing the virus spread of slave freeing. Mr. Garrison was going on a triumphant tour of England as the chief spokesman for the American slave. But some were afraid he'd have to sneak in and out of New York because of angry mobs. A convention was planned by the Quakers of Philadelphia, to form a great national antislavery society. The New York Antislave Committee and the Boston Abolition Committee were expected to join. Right in Canterbury, could there one day be a small antislavery society? The two women continued to discuss the exciting possibility.

Something else Miss Crandall told Hester, and Hester now confided to Bernadette: a widower minister of the Baptist church named Calvin Philleo had met Miss Crandall at her first trial and was writing to her. The minister lived in Ithaca with his teen-aged daughter. His admiraton was apparently not confined to the teacher's work with the blacks.

How wonderful it would be if Prudence had a strong shoulder to lean on in these hard days. Hester sighed.

"With the Canterbury sheriff ordered to arrest her sister, I don't see how Miss Crandall keeps up her spirits. But she manages. She's even planned her Exhibition Day for next Saturday, Bernadette. I've promised her you'll be there . . ."

The rising sharp wind quickened Bernadette's hike to the village.

In the school yard, beech trees shone vivid yellow; the maple would soon be crimson. Bernadette opened the gate in the white rail fence and skirted the fountain, whose bubbles sparkled and leaped no longer because water hauled by wagon was too precious for decoration.

She knocked at the black-shuttered front door. Miriam and Eliza opened it. Miriam curtsied, gave Bernadette a special smile, and motioned her into a handsome large hall.

Bernadette's first impression was of dark angels. Everywhere she looked black girls flitted in gauzy white dresses.

"Miss Almira made them," Miriam explained, lifting her arm to show off the full sleeve. "She stayed up a lot of nights stitching."

For the first time, Bernadette went into the parlor, the grandest she had ever been in: high ceilings, high draped windows through which the sun streamed, an elegant mantel . . .

"You've never seen anything but hallway and kitchen, have you?" Miriam remembered. "Come look at the rest with me."

Miriam showed off parlor and dining room, library and morning room, and kitchen. Then they climbed the backstairs to the big ell and the girls' sleeping rooms. Miriam motioned to the four bedrooms in the house proper. "Miss Crandall has the front one and her sister another."

Downstairs they walked among desks which crowded the library and the sunny morning room facing the Plainfield Road. Each desk had a quill standing upright in a bottle of real ink. On the walls hung an astronomy chart, a small whatnot crowded with shells and stones, several engravings of houses and bridges which Miriam said the older girls copied in art lessons, and a map of the world in soft colors.

Avidly Bernadette studied desks and displays. Miriam watched Bernadette's hungry face, a wistful smile hovering on her lips.

"Young ladies, young ladies . . ." Miss Almira made little clapping gestures with her hands, rounding up the white-clad girls.

In the parlor to which they returned, Bernadette observed

that the adults had broken up their chatting groups and now sought settles and chairs. Before Miriam left to join her schoolmates, the black girl hurriedly pointed out these spectators: Arnold Buffum, antislavery agent; the friendly Bensons from Brooklyn; saintly Reverend Samuel May — "he tells us stories"; the nondescript profile which belonged to Arthur Tappan, the rich backer from New York. (Mr. Tappan looked very ordinary to be so rich, she thought. But *very* stern . . .)

"Mr. Garrison would have come but he's in England," Miriam whispered, then hurried off.

There was an unnamed adult Bernadette spotted. He was a big, broad-shouldered, middle-aged man with a lined, sober face and auburn hair with a striking silver streak through it. She wondered why Miriam had neglected to say who this noticeable gentleman was . . .

With the girls crowding the hall door and lined up outside it, the program commenced. A blessing was rendered in a forceful voice by Reverend Kneeland. The school and Miss Crandall were forthrightly called to God's attention, and God was reminded that persecution was aflame in Canterbury.

Sarah Harris, the girl who had started Miss Crandall on her perilous venture, then stepped forth to recite. Out came a long admonition to young ladies by Hannah More which Bernadette privately assessed as starchy, poky, and undaring.

In a trembling voice, Emila Wilson read her own composition on friendship. Miriam followed, racing through a dutiful essay on obedience. Bernadette chuckled inwardly because she knew what a struggle Miriam had had composing an essay on that subject. "Miss Crandall says it's for my own good," Miriam had complained darkly.

When Ann Eliza spoke on forgiveness, Bernadette listened to every word. Ann Eliza was a saint, Miriam often declared in mystification. Hearing the sweet, melodious, sincere voice, Bernadette believed it.

Piano pieces tinkled; in singsong voices, the younger girls reviewed reading, arithmetic, and spelling.

Bernadette was thoroughly relaxed by now and wished Exhibition Day would go on forever. The sunny beauty of the house, her warm-hearted black friends' earnest, familiar, expressive faces, the smiling, approving spectators, the straightforward simplicity of the two Crandall sisters, the heady aroma of spiced cider and tarts cooking, all conspired to make Bernadette feel at home. A different sort of home, but a place to belong, nevertheless.

A place to belong . . .

The truth welled up in her, overwhelming her.

When the program was finished, Eliza Henley proudly showed her the journals each girl kept. And it was Eliza who told Bernadette the name of the big, auburn-haired man. "That's the Reverend Calvin Philleo," she murmured with raised eyebrows. Bernadette turned a swift, embarrassed look on this remarkably romantic object — Miss Crandall's admirer.

"He was a minister in Suffield and Pawtucket and once was apprenticed to a blacksmith."

"Will they marry, do you think?" Ann asked Bernadette. There were four of them, heads together, ostensibly bent over Eliza's journal but really whispering in intimate excitement about the Reverend.

"Well, girls, and what might you be speaking of?" Miss Almira asked pleasantly, coming into the morning room. "Cups need filling in the parlor. Come along — I'll help you place them on the trays."

As they trooped into the kitchen behind Almira Crandall, her blood began an agitated pounding in Bernadette's head. Maybe it would be easier just to ask Miss Almira . . .

Miriam, Ann, Emila, and Bernadette gathered around the kitchen table while Miss Almira poured cider into the cups.

"Emila brought the cider to the school, Bernadette," Almira Crandall commented pleasantly. "The girls often bring food from home now, it being so hard to come by in Canterbury."

Bernadette's voice sounded faintly. "Miss Crandall, would you let me come to your seminary?"

There was a long, breathless silence. Bernadette was painfully aware of the amazed dark eyes turned to her. All but Miriam's. Miriam's eyes went soft enough for tears.

"*Would* you go here?" the astonished Miss Almira asked at last.

"Yes. I need to learn because I want to go to college. Besides, Miriam is my closest friend and she's acquainting me with lots of the other girls."

Almira resumed the pouring, her face a study. When she spoke, it was with evident difficulty. "No, Bernadette, we couldn't take you in our school, though I rejoice you have the courage to ask it of us. You can't imagine how Canterbury would make you suffer. Six months ago I couldn't have imagined either."

"She could live here with us," Miriam challenged.

"No, I don't suppose I could," Bernadette amended honestly. "The Frys expected me to be a day student — they're cheaper."

"The cups are filled. Take them into the parlor, all but Bernadette . . ."

Even Miriam went, though with open reluctance. Bernadette and Miss Almira were left alone by the table.

"Bernadette, my sister goes on second trial in just a few weeks. It would enrage her enemies even more if we taught a white girl here with blacks."

"I shouldn't want to hurt Miss Crandall."

"I know you wouldn't. For your sake, for her sake, please try to understand why I must tell you no."

"Yes, Miss Crandall. I guess I understand. But if you don't mind, it's getting dark and I have a long walk home, so I think I'll go out the kitchen door. I thank you for asking me; I'll thank Miss Crandall later . . ."

"Bernadette . . ."

Miss Almira Crandall started around the table, but Bernadette didn't want any sympathetic touching which would bring the tears sooner than they were bound to fall.

She ran all the way home because she'd forgotten her shawl.

In all the long months she'd wrestled with attending the black seminary, it never occurred to her she'd ask and be refused. Her whole world felt as though it was tumbling down around her with a crash. Was there no one, nowhere — no help at all?

The stars glittered brightly and distantly.

Next day she asked Hester Fry if — work permitting — she could go to common school fall term.

"Common school! But you know everything they teach there!"

"Yes, ma'am. Still, I expect it wouldn't hurt to learn it twice."

"Our brother Fry would like to have you come back to live with him in Ohio. He'd tutor you till you're sixteen and he thinks you might be able to take the regular college program that way. But now your Aunt Leah suddenly wants you to come home to their farm instead — says now you're old enough to help her. And I, I'm trying to convince your Uncle Marcus to let you attend Miss Beecher's fine female seminary in Hartford. If I had the dower I came to marriage with, you'd be at Hartford tomorrow. Till everything's untangled, of course you can go to common school, child. Naturally you can."

chapter 19

⁑⁑⁑⁑⁑⁑⁑⁑⁑

Passing the barn door, Bernadette waved to Paul, who was flailing beans, the red seeds jumping wildly in all directions. Paul threw down the flail and joined her.

"Where you going?"

"Into the village."

"To run an errand for Ma?"

"I left my good shawl at the schoolmarm's and I'm going to fetch it back this afternoon."

"I'll trot in with you then. My arms are pulled out of their sockets flailing beans. Besides, I've already done more than Pa asked me to do."

"Well, I may stay at the school a minute," Bernadette warned.

"I'll hang out at the store till you're finished."

But unaccountably, Paul tagged along to the seminary.

Miriam came out with Bernadette's shawl over her arm. She barely gave Paul a nod. "Can you sit in the carriage shed a little while before you go back?"

"I guess so . . ."

Paul Fry trudged beside them stubbornly. Why in the world *is* he tagging along? Bernadette wondered, nonplussed, as the three of them crossed the backyard to the big carriage house with its churning black weather vane.

Miriam leaned on an empty feeding trough. "Every week," she said, producing a sheaf of papers, "I'm going to write down for you what we study."

"But that's lots of extra work!"

"Do me good." Miriam half laughed. "You'd be surprised how much better you learn when it's for someone else. And I'll get in practice for teaching my sister."

"For pity sake, Bernadette, I could write down all them — those — things I learn at the academy," Paul chimed in. "You don't have to get it from this place."

"I'm ever so obliged, Paul, and I'll take anything you bring me. But I'm obliged to Miriam, too . . ."

"I heard Miss Prudence and Miss Almira talking about your asking to go to our school," Miriam confided. "At first Miss Prudence, she was determined to take you in. Then Almira reminded her you couldn't live here and you'd have to come and go past all the village houses and the store and Miss Almira said — judging by what happened to me — it wouldn't be safe. Do you know what they've done to a black boys' school up in New Hampshire? The village folk yoked oxen to the building and hauled it into a swamp."

"They couldn't do a thing like that to this big house . . ."

"Bernadette!" Paul's voice, interrupting, was like a whiplash. "Did you ask to go to this school?"

"Yes. Last Saturday at the Exhibition Day. But Miss Almira Crandall told me no."

"So you dragged our name down by asking and then trampled on us altogether by getting refused! Does Pa know?"

"No, nor your ma, either. When the answer was no, what was the use of raising a fuss?"

"You did me a favor," Paul swore, "so I'll button my lips for you about this. But I'm done! I came in today thinking I might learn for myself what you and Ma see in these niggers. Well, I'll have you know, I don't see *anything* in them. I'm glad the house was rotten-egged after the Exhibition Day. I'm real glad . . ."

He turned on his heel and strode across the browning grass.

"Paul Fry," Miriam called softly, "did you do the rotten-egging?"

"I wouldn't lower myself!" was all Paul shot over his shoulder before he skirted the house foundations, dipped down to the Plainfield Road, and disappeared.

"He'd be a better boy if he kept better company," Miriam observed.

"Still, I can't make myself believe he'd go so much against his mother and rotten-egg the school, Miriam. He says he crawls into the cider mill. I guess I have to believe it till I get proof of something else." There was a great tired heaviness in Bernadette, watching Paul stalk away. She didn't even feel like lingering with Miriam. Lamps were lit in the schoolhouse; the soft warm gold from the windows didn't include her.

"I have to get home."

"I wrote a composition this week just for you." Miriam spoke softly. "I wanted to write a story as interesting as Hannibal and the Romans, then I realized Beeljie's was the only interesting story I knew. So I finished the story of my grandmother for you."

Wordlessly, Bernadette hugged Miriam; Miriam gave her a bear hug back.

"Good night, Bernadette," called Ann, sticking her head out the upstairs ell window.

"Good night . . ."

"My grandmother, Beeljie the Foulah princess, lived for five weeks in a slave pen or barracoon on the edge of the ocean. Grandmother said many Negroes had never seen the ocean and were terrified, thinking it some great beast.

"There were about two hundred females in her pen. At the end of each barred and thatched barracoon were watch-houses where sentinels stood with muskets.

"The barracoon was part of a factory or village made up of slavers and traders. Beeljie remembers her factory had watchtowers, storerooms and kitchens, a rice house, a depot for water, and a square where sometimes after dinner the slaves drummed or danced, although Beeljie did not. Cannons pointed into the factory. Beeljie waited; she wasn't sure for what.

"But finally one morning, she saw what she waited for. A great, fat-bellied monster, a canoe larger than the largest canoe in all the world with tall spires and huge white wings, rested on the Afric waters when she looked out her barred window.

"Boatmen called Kroomen pulled up their long dugout canoes onto the white sands. Women were herded from their pens while the men were driven from the men's barracoons. People fell down hugging the sands of their homeland but were bound hand and foot and dragged into the boats by Kroomen and traders with hippopotamus-hide whips. Though Beeljie didn't know the language of most of the women, she thought they were fearful they would be carried across the water to be eaten. Some tried to throw themselves into the high surf, but Beeljie did not try to kill herself, for now she had been sold, she wanted fiercely to live. Nor did she think she would be eaten, for who would go through such heavy waters for such a purpose? Fires would be lit on the beach, instead.

"Not crying or moaning, my grandmother sat upright and hated the white-winged canoe. The wind, coming downwind, carried its smell. Beeljie had scorn for a canoe which would let itself smell like that.

"All naked, the men were shackled two by two, the right wrist and ankle of one to the left of another. Then they were attached to the great chain that ran on both sides of the ship. The women were left free of chains but like the men were later taken to lower decks. The women were laid in rows and there were so many of them they had to double their legs to make room for others. The ceilings were so low there wasn't room to sit up straight. The day of loading no one was allowed on deck for fear of mutiny, for mutinies happened most often while shore was in sight. My grandmother, the Foulah, learned this from a Coromantee who knew a little Foulah; they spoke with each other over the heads of the others. The Coromantee woman was the only woman my grandmother admired. The rest of the women sniffled cravenly and made a continuous moaning outcry.

"The slaves were fed twice that day — horse beans, to Beeljie's disgust — and half a pint of water served in a pannikin. In the night the ship made fearful creaks and groans and Beeljie sensed it was sailing away.

"Next morning after breakfast, she and the others were

herded on deck. The sky was blue and bright but there was no sight of land — water was everywhere.

"There was now a practice which happened every day. All were ordered to stand up and make jerking or jiggling motions. The men slaves jumped in their irons until their ankles bled while sailors paraded among them with cat-o'-nine tails. Later Beeljie and the Coromantee understood why they danced to the beat of the upturned kettle. If some were not set in motion they would hunch down, hang their heads and — perfectly still — refuse food and thus die in a few days. It was not good to watch crewmen mistreat grieving women who refused to eat. Beeljie saw a shovel of coals placed so near a woman's lips she was burned; some were flogged. There was something else — a legged instrument — which was designed especially to force a fasting slave to eat. It was hammered between clenched teeth.

"While the slaves ate and danced, their sleeping rooms were scraped and swabbed. Beeljie learned why it was that the downwind carried such a foul smell.

"In late afternoon the slaves got their last meal, horse beans again. Beeljie said the bean paste was hated so much the women and men threw it in each other's faces when the crew wasn't watching. After the second meal, all had to go below . . . spoon fashion they were once more laid out to spend the night groaning and quarreling.

"When it rained, Beeljie and the rest were not allowed on deck. Beeljie was lucky and had only two days of stormy weather which she spent below. It was so hot these days, slaves near the gratings saw steam rising out of it. Many fevers and much sickness followed those two days below deck. Slaves who died were thrown overboard as though they were nothing but refuse. My grandmother thought flux, fever, or fixed melancholy killed a great number, but later she learned few were lost in comparison to other dirty and tight-packed slave ships.

"The last two or three days of the passage the slaves were released from their irons. To fatten them they were given bigger meals and more than the hated horse beans.

"They came to Jamaica. The men slaves were placed on the main deck, the women the quarter-deck. A gun had sounded and white men soon began to come out to the ship by skiff. The purchasers rushed around the decks like beasts of prey, encircling those slaves they wished to buy. The women cried dreadfully. Now, at last, they were to be eaten, they thought.

"Grandmother was bought in Jamaica for a personal maid to a planter's wife. This planter's American wife grew so homesick for Charleston, her husband remained in Jamaica only two years before he took his family home. My grandmother never lived in a field slave's shack, never pinched a cotton worm, never broke her back chopping cotton at dawn.

"But my grandfather lived like that. He was an enormous Coromantee man, so tall and thin and agile folks mistook him for an Indian. He came to the plantation cheap-bought because he was scarred by floggings from trying to escape. Planters didn't want a runaway man. But Beeljie's owner was a canny man and he sized up my grandfather for what he was and put him to work overseeing his own. None of the cotton slaves disobeyed my grandfather twice. Still it was not his black whip which made them mind; it was the stern fire in his eyes.

"But bad times came to the Georgia planter and as he sold his land he sold his slaves. My grandparents were among the last to go. Beeljie had borne the Coromantee six children. All brought extra prices at the red-flagged Charleston slave market.

"I don't have the taste for writing any more about Beeljie except to finish by saying she was lucky past compare when the same Rhode Island family bought her and my grandfather together. Later they had two more children and kept them.

"This is not a pretty story, not half pretty enough for Miss Prudence Crandall or the girls at school. The girls at school don't pretend to know where they came from and wouldn't ever put down words as plain as mine.

"But what can you say if the truth be plain?"

chapter 20

✝✝✝✝✝✝✝✝✝

Davɪᴅ ᴀɴɴᴏᴜɴᴄᴇᴅ ungraciously he'd take off a day from work and drive Hester to the trial in Brooklyn. If the whole country was going to be there, even at harvest time, he supposed they might as well crowd in, too. Then he revealed his real purpose: he wanted Hester to hear the most responsible men of Connecticut declare the black school illegal and Mistress Prudence Crandall an insolent and insupportable nuisance.

From the comfort of the chaise, Bernadette could survey Brooklyn as she couldn't have from Ingo's nag. Brooklyn, seat of Windham County, was a white mosaic of houses, jail, lawns, taverns, stores, along with a courthouse, a printing office, and a fifty-year-old meetinghouse with a slender spire topped by a gilded weathercock. David said its yellowing maples had been planted by the Revolutionary War hero, General Israel Putnam.

In the courthouse, the plain little courtroom was packed and suffocating in Indian-summer heat. Outside the open windows, late locusts whirred, droning a serenade. Black-coated men and petticoated women helplessly fried in their own fat. Foreheads glistened, handkerchiefs mopped, upper lips gleamed. Spectators tolerated their neighbors' smells and tried to believe they had none of their own.

On a raised dais Prudence Crandall sat straight as a ramrod on a chair facing the jury. On the high box above her leaned Judge David Daggett, Chief Justice of the Supreme Court. On each side of the room the opposing counsels faced each other at opposite tables. Bernadette thought Prosecutor Andrew Judson's expression this morning was especially rancorous. It must be making him more sour every day to stare out of his house windows right at the black seminary. Mr. Welch, Mr. Cleaveland, and Mr. Bulkeley, important Connecticut statesmen, conferred with Mr. Judson, whose jowls trembled with his vigorous head-shaking.

At the other table were Miss Crandall's own lawyers, the best men in Connecticut Pastor May had been able to hire with Mr. Arthur Tappan's ten thousand dollars. There was no question Mr. Goddard, Mr. Strong, and Mr. Ellsworth were more humane than their opponents, Bernadette concluded. Just look at their expressions . . .

While she cast a weather eye at the awed and solemn jury in its box, Judge Daggett brought down his gavel. Even the locusts paused respectfully in their droning.

"The prosecution," Judge Daggett said, "may proceed."

Andrew Judson rose from his chair.

With rapt attention, Bernadette listened to the furnace of heated legalism which smoldered and erupted all day.

The prosecution referred repeatedly to the new black law of Connecticut passed specifically to put Miss Crandall down: ". . . no person shall set up or establish in this state any school . . . for the instruction . . . of colored persons who are not inhabitants of this state . . . without the consent . . . of the selectmen of the town . . ."

Then Mr. Judson spoke again: "A white person coming

from another county can be made a citizen by naturalization but a black one cannot." His statement was followed by the prosecution's summary. "Congress was not mistaken when they supposed the spirit of the Constitution gave to white persons alone the right to citizenship. Indians are not citizens — never can be made citizens. Why? They are persons of color. The proud term 'American citizen' means something more than a slave — it means a white man who can enjoy the highest honor of the republic, the privilege of choosing his rulers, and being one himself.

"This is not the case of the town of Canterbury, alone, against Prudence Crandall; it is the case of the state of Connecticut, and every town, however remote, and every citizen, however unconcerned. Let the black laws be pronounced unconstitutional and a corresponding school for males will be established in some other town. The law is made for the preservation of our state. Resistance to it is solely for the purpose of sowing seeds of disquiet in the South. Let it not be said that a jury in Windham County commenced the word of dissolving the Union . . ."

Bernadette, mesmerized, probed the words, at last understanding them. And at last she committed herself wholeheartedly, not just to special people she'd grown to love, but to a cause.

Meanwhile, beside her, David nodded vigorously for the prosecution, his expression grave, and Hester sat quiet and attentive. Feelings were mirrored in the faces of the jurors, in the triumphant or discomforted whispers and rustles of the spectators, in partisan snorts and snickers which erupted now and again and made the stern judge frown. For hours Prudence Crandall sat nearly motionless, the stain of moisture growing around the back of her armpits the only telltale sign of her proud suffering. The locusts droned, now soothingly, now angrily, as though they, too, were chorus to the court drama.

Bernadette thought the defense was brilliant even if brief. Goddard, Strong, and Ellsworth spoke in turn, producing facts from history and legal opinion in the United States and England on the unconstitutionality of the black laws. The defense stubbornly held to its stand, based on the Declaration of Independence, that Negroes were citizens and entitled to citizens' rights.

Both sides finished their arguments. "Why should a man be educated who can't be a freedman?" shouted Andrew Judson.

"Connecticut cannot withhold from citizens the rights they enjoy in other states," was the stern reply.

Judge Daggett made his charge to the jury, that same Judge Daggett who, two years ago, had caused the dissolution of a Negro boys' school: "It would be a perversion of terms . . . to say that blacks, free blacks or Indians, were citizens . . . I am bound by my duty, to say they are not citizens . . ."

Bernadette watched Prudence Crandall's friends, who sat with Almira in a cluster as near to the defendant's chair as they could get. The warm, rock-firm Reverend Sam May, who believed so utterly in all humankind that he was able to fall asleep in the room of a dangerous madman; the dying Reverend Kneeland of Packerville; George Benson taking notes for *The Liberator;* beside him, Charles Burleigh scribbling away for *The Unionist;* the young teacher, William Burleigh, sitting beside his brother Charles.

166

When the jury came back, there wasn't a sound. Even the locusts waited.

"Your Honor," said the foreman, "we find the defendant guilty . . . "

Bernadette felt a stunning shock pass through her; it was as though she'd been physically hit by something. She looked into Hester's dismayed face. And then glanced beyond to David, whose look was the same as a barn cat after it had finished a big plate of cream. You could almost see milk on David's whiskers.

"Well, Wife" — David rose, stretched — "gather up the baby and let's go home."

"I'd like to speak with the teacher first."

"No indeed, we've no time for that. Besides, as you can see, she's already occupied with her friends."

Defying David Fry, Bernadette slipped up, briefly joined the outer circle of folks excitedly gathered around Miss Crandall and her attorneys. She lingered only a moment for she knew David would have plenty to say about her insubordination. But she remained long enough to hear that the defense planned to file a bill of exceptions and make an appeal to the Connecticut Court of Errors.

"We'll see that you and the school get a fair trial yet," Mr. Goddard assured her. "We'll fight this case to the state's highest tribunal."

"Meantime, she must still live under a bond?"

"Oh, yes," was an answer which rumbled from the broad-shouldered, red-haired suitor, Calvin Philleo.

Bernadette fled down the aisle to join Hester and David at the crowded doorway.

David Fry felt too good to scold her for running up to Miss

Crandall. All the way home, he lectured his wife about the justice of the court's decision.

"Now maybe we can get rid of this misery, and Canterbury can return to calm."

"Calm things," Hester finally remarked soberly, "aren't always right things."

Bernadette couldn't understand how Hester could seem so contained. For herself, she was mad. Mad clean through. Ready to fight in any way she could.

She started her fight that very night by an impassioned letter to Pastor Fry telling him about the trial. More than anyone in the world, she wanted Pastor Fry to understand Prudence Crandall. And she wanted him to see Miriam and the black girls as she knew them to be.

But if he didn't, she would disagree.

chapter 21

†††††††††

No LONGER did Bernadette and Hester push their way to Quaker Meeting through thick corn stalks. Instead, they walked on the stalks' stubble through wide, clear fields. Signs of winter multiplied. The cut corn was shocked in tepees, drying brown. Brilliant orange pumpkins and squash were piled against barn foundations, their tangly vines left behind to wither in the fields. The frosts had come, and breathtaking vermillion leaves had floated downward, slowly, dreamlike, to lie on the ground in dimming heaps. The earth had hardened and the wet bogs no longer coated their shoes with mud. Finally, inexorably, the first swirl of snowflakes exploded out of a heavy sky. The snow made only a fine sifting on the ground, but David looked as lowery as the clouds when Bernadette and Hester set out for Meeting, the baby wrapped in every blanket Hester possessed.

"It's not deep; we can manage," Hester insisted. But Bernadette was saddened. She knew, and Hester knew, the drifts would soon be too deep.

Finally winter closed them in altogether. One blizzard followed another and the meadow below the house lay white, crossed in the feeble glow of the sun with deep blue shadows. The snow roller, pulled by six horses, creaked up the narrow road to the farm. Its two big barrels pressed out the tracks the farm cutters and sleds required. The snow roller was new to the township and David was proud of it. He explained to Bernadette that the idea for it came from the huge hogsheads of tobacco rolled down through the great White Mountain notches of New Hampshire.

Each time the roadmaster swung the snow roller into the farmyard and made a big circle, Hester went out with turnovers for the driver and his youthful crew. Young boys rode, whooping and hollering, on the rig, and were needed to knock the icy balls from the horses' hoofs.

When the winds howled and the world was blurred with whirling whiteness, the nearby common school closed its doors. Bernadette didn't feel bad. Dutifully she had plodded off to the one-room school, but she would sit amidst strange faces in stifling heat or ensuing cold and learn nothing beyond what she'd already been taught. The big boys made her head ache with their poking and heehawing, and the near-blind old teacher, just passing through the village this year, had difficulty shouting them down. Yet he was too feeble to throw them out and bar the door against them.

A grumbling Paul attended the boys' academy. To hear Paul talk, he was the most put-upon creature in Connecticut for having to study.

By candlelight Bernadette continued to memorize Miriam's books, though her room grew so cold that even with the feather bed and the heated flannel-wrapped maple chunks, she finally couldn't bear to hold the books outside the covers. Inviting disaster, she would set the candle right next to her pillow.

In the winter she had time for long thoughts, thoughts

about what lay ahead for her if she never had a chance to live any other life than that of a countrywoman.

Would there be thirst? Every drop of water would have to be hauled, whether by sweep, windlass, or pump.

Would there be heat? Cold? If there were cold, high shallow firepits yawned in the farmhouse rooms, requiring split logs from the woodpile, logs which had to be lugged by the young or the female, by those not engaged in the field or barns. In the heat of summer, the lug poles and cranes would bristle on the hearth where heavy pots would hang, to be stirred by blistered hands and watched by burning faces.

Would there be hunger? Yes, hunger always, and not just in the summer when the kitchen garden must be hoed, weeded, and harvested, but in the lean winter months, too. Bernadette grew tired summarizing in her mind the food preserving. The cellar shelves groaned with jugs of cherries, blueberries, preserves, plums, jams, pickles — how many pickled things there were! The shelves were monuments to hours of toil. The cellar bins were full: apples, potatoes, carrots, beets, knotty winter cabbages stored in fresh sand. Barrels and crocks were filled with salt pork, mincemeat, corned beef, salt fish. Eggs sat in earthen jars of water glass waiting the chickens' new laying time. Cider must be brewed, medicines made from barks and berries, eggs hunted, even milk gotten when Paul and David stayed late in the timothy and clover fields. Butter was churned, bread baked; on Saturday Hester spent most of the day pounding and kneading on the cherry-top table. Oh, there was much else Bernadette could add up about food, but if she did she would permanently lose her appetite.

At least she felt there was hope in clothes. In Ohio, Pastor's wife still spent the fall and winter preparing the wool fibers, spinning them into thread, weaving the thread on the cumbersome, perverse handmade monster of a loom while Bernadette crouched beside her and passed up the proper colored thread to fit the pattern. But in Connecticut Hester said she would buy her yard goods in the store, since they were growing so plentiful and reasonably priced, and David was so anxious to sell the sheep's wool to the cloth factories springing up on every New England milldam. Except for feather beds, quilts, rag rugs, clothes sewing, knitting, and constant mending, Hester was planning her freedom from the wheel and loom.

But clothes must be kept clean. That meant the baby's, too. Tubs were filled with boiling water and stirred with long-handled forks. There was starch to make, and learning to wield the black flatirons Bernadette had once found so hard to lift.

The big house must be kept spotless. That meant the broom and the cloth, the scouring of brown-board tables and splintery floor, the beating, lugging, and grubbing in dusty corners.

They had to make tallow dips and candles for light; they had to make their own soap.

Baby nurturing and tending . . . many women couldn't even get to church, being left behind with the little ones while the rest of the family crowded into a church-bound wagon.

But what was there for a woman to look forward to when she did finish her work? Hester was too far from neighbors to run over and chat. She saw mostly Neighbor Shaw, the hired men, the peddler. There were occasional quilting bees, a harvest supper or two, but not many raisings anymore, with all the land taken up. Besides, Hester sighed, getting ready for raisings meant so much mountainous food preparation she was dead by the time the day came.

Before she'd stopped going to church, Hester had always liked village church meetings, the May missionary meetings, the prayer meetings — they were her main joy. Such meetings seemed very sober to Bernadette.

But it wasn't the work — everyone expected to work hard — so much as it was the imprisonment.

Most of all, Bernadette and Hester minded being shut away from the news. Oh, Canterbury gossip came to them: there were thirty-two girls at the black school now; a visiting pastor had not been allowed to preach in Canterbury's church because he had stopped off at the school; in a crisis, drugs had been refused once more — but both hungered for news of a wider world, the news which Prudence Crandall and Miriam had supplied, the news which *The Liberator* carried.

Antislavery news . . .

Still, David had forbade the newspaper, and Hester, his wife, must accept his forbidding. If David hadn't feared God's speaking to Hester, he'd never have allowed Black Hill. David didn't care if Bernadette got any more schooling. And Bernadette had to abide his indifference.

If a woman had so little to say in it all, wherein was she different from the mule at the mill? Bernadette wondered. Around and around the mule went, at someone else's behest.

What lay ahead for Bernadette?

Restlessly, she put down her knitting, went to the window, and watched a turkey buzzard wheeling slowly, purposefully, above the meadow.

The bird seemed to speak to her. Be free, be free!

But how?

chapter 22

✝✝✝✝✝✝✝✝✝

ONE MORNING RACHEL rocked on her hands and knees. Then all of a sudden, the rocking gained momentum and the baby crept, quiet as a mouse in her new discovery. During the next few days, she grew increasingly proficient at tucking her legs under her and managing arms and legs in crablike tandem. She began to crawl everywhere.

Suddenly dangers sprang up all over, especially near the fiery hearth.

It was good Bernadette was out of school this wintry morning — Rachel had already unwound Hester's tatting and gotten a splinter in her hand from the box of kindling.

To keep her out of trouble, Bernadette picked her up and stood her in her lap. Rachel patted Bernadette's cheek, pulled her nose, and put her face in Bernadette's hair, giggling uproariously from the tickle. She was impishly round faced, with dark blue eyes and what the family unknowingly felt was God-given curly black hair. Hester said Rachel was one of the fey Irish Frys turning up at last.

While Hester wasn't looking, Bernadette spat on her fingers and brushed Rachel's hair up on the nape of her neck. Automatically spitting and rubbing, spitting and rubbing, Bernadette had earned her reward in the soft, short ringlets through which she now poked a wondering finger. Well, what if she had helped God a little!

Hester turned away from loading the brick oven with bread.

Bernadette put the baby down; on her immobilized feet Rachel hung on to the settle for dear life.

"At least she's anchored," Hester observed indulgently.

Like a careful old man, Rachel began to foot her way around the settle. But for once Bernadette wasn't really watching the baby. Her own wintry wonderment at what women were and must do hadn't ended just in visions of jugs lined up on groaning food shelves. There were other questions, too, questions it seemed impossible to ask anyone, questions it was evil even to think about.

Absently, Bernadette helped Rachel move from rung to rung, her spirits in a quandary. Was she wicked for wondering? How could anyone not wonder about the rest of it, after what had happened when Rachel was born?

Bernadette sighed; she was used to thinking of herself as a little evil now — defiance being evil. But she guessed she was hardier than fashionably delicate young ladies were about their wickedness. Besides, to Bernadette there seemed to be a lot of ignorance which went along with evil, and a lot of giggly nonsense.

Still, could she really ask Hester?

Hester's profile at the oven was tender and trustworthy. There was a forthrightness in Hester . . .

Even with her courage summoned up to the final notch, it was a low desperate voice which came out of Bernadette. "Ma'am, sometimes it seems so deep to me — what I am, what lies ahead. When my time-of-the-month came in Ohio, Mrs. Fry said I must prepare for womanhood. But she didn't say how I should prepare. It frightens me. Do most girls

176

cry in the night because they don't understand?"

Hester paused, startled, but seemed to sense instantly what Bernadette's question meant. "Why, dear child, you haven't a mother to take your troubles to, have you? And the first experience you had with us was troubling."

"Yes," Bernadette admitted, looking hard at her hands. "It troubles me, but at least I can speak of it now. And at least I learned what it was to be born. But what I don't understand is, how does a child come to be? I know it has something to do with the father; the girls whisper of that. But none knows exactly."

Hester might be tender, trustworthy, forthright, but now her face turned scarlet. She came to the settle and sat down. Bernadette murmured contritely, "I'm sorry. If you can't tell me, I'll understand."

"I'll try to tell you," Hester struggled determinedly. "Yes, the baby *is* there because of the father. The father and mother come together and it is from this coming together that a baby begins."

"I see," Bernadette answered at last. "I didn't know whether it was the same for us as for animals."

"I wouldn't confuse the act of animals with human coupling, Bernadette. That makes of it flesh and no feeling, and it's love that is its essence," Hester countered soberly. She went on, "When the father's seed joins an egg in the mother's body, a baby starts, at first only a cell or two, but month by month growing until it becomes truly human. It takes nine months. The child is formed, and the womb expels the child."

"There's work and pain to expel, isn't there, and sometimes the mother or baby dies?"

177

"Work and pain, yes, though not always so long or so hard as what you saw upstairs. And more times than not, the mother and child live to be happy together, to enjoy their love for each other."

The long silence which flowed between them was growing warm and easy. Rachel sat on the floor and clattered a measuring spoon lustily.

"Then if you wanted six children, six times the seed would be planted in you?"

Hester got up, opened the oven door, unaccountably slammed it shut without testing the bread. To Bernadette's astonishment, when she wiped her hands on her apron, they seemed to be trembling. But Bernadette had never sensed anyone so determined to tell the truth. It was a lesson in life that Bernadette in gratitude never meant to forget.

"Many more times than the number of their children a man and woman lie together," Hester said. "To be together in that way shows tenderness, caring."

What had seemed clear to Bernadette, turned confused. She tried asking another way: "One of the girls at the school in Ohio told me wedded women lived in dread of bearing babies, said her own mother prayed not to have another child. But this girl said it was a woman's Christian duty — how the baby is got and how it's born. That makes it sound dreadful."

"Many women *are* burdened with too many children," Hester agreed quietly. "And they are burdened with that frightened feeling. But I can only say, in my life I was not burdened by that fear and certainly I was not burdened by an overabundance of children."

Bernadette sat in a brown study, piecing together what

she'd heard. Well, if this last part wasn't entirely clear, it would suffice until later. "After the birth's all over, it must be wonderful to have a child," she observed simply, out of an opening heart.

"You forget the work and pain almost within minutes, Bernadette. Next to the love of a good husband, a child's the most wonderful thing God gives us. I hope you'll remember that."

Hester's face wore a noble serenity now, not unmindful of suffering but accepting of it for gain far greater. Rachel rapped the spoon on the floor, hummed, "Ma . . . Ma . . . Mmmmm . . ."

Love from both mother and child seemed to reach out and enfold Bernadette. She got up from the bench, poked the fire log.

"I don't feel sad or upset anymore," she confided cheerfully. "I'm going to be a schoolteacher, have my own school, because I want to be free and take care of myself. Still," she concluded dreamily, "when I'm growing old, maybe I won't mind marrying if someone will have me."

Hester's lips curved convulsively in a secret little smile. "You might not be so old and, no, you might not even mind," she added casually. Then she jumped up. "Lord have mercy on us, child, we've burnt our bread!"

chapter 23

✝✝✝✝✝✝✝✝

The frosty limbs of the tree cracked against the wall by his window as Paul leaped lightly onto a slender branch and slid to the one below.

No question about it, he knew every foothold by heart. Only trouble was, he was getting sick of his nighttime excursions into town.

Good and sick of it on a night like this: cold as an ice house, it was. But no snow, and that's why Ingo had lingered by the academy and caught Paul coming out, even though Paul had tried to stick with Abner and Charlie and pretend not to see Ingo.

With his fur earmuffs down and his hands in his knit mittens, Paul ran till his chest ached with his breathing. But still he couldn't keep himself halfway warm. The wind bit into him, that's what. Thank goodness, going home he'd be running with the wind to his back. He wished he were running home . . .

He nosed his way into the Lewises' dark barn. Ingo wasn't sitting smoking a cigar tonight; he was standing right inside the big door, waiting. Coming out of the blackness, his voice made Paul jump.

"Paul? That you?"

"Well, it's not your pa. Where are the rest? Scared out on a night like this?"

"Nah," Ingo answered, unmoving. "I didn't ask them to come tonight."

"Why not? What fun will the two of us have ringing the school bell?"

"Well, I just *mentioned* we might do that, you and I. I didn't say for certain that's what we'd do."

"Ingo," Paul said sharply, "it's bitter as a blizzard out there. And I'm sleepy. I been up late these nights studying."

"Studying! What you doing *that* for?"

"Oh, I been studying some things for Bernadette, passing them on to her."

"Guess you're not mad at her anymore for going to the Quakers with your ma. Guess you don't think folks are gossipin' that your ma's queer for not going to church with your pa . . ."

"I didn't say all that," Paul answered impatiently, taking his mittens off, blowing on his fingers. "Let's not talk. Let's just go. It'll take some doing to get up on the school roof without losing our footing."

"Maybe too much doing . . ." Ingo just kept on standing inside the barn door.

"Well, doing or no doing, are we going to try it? Ingo, I got a *long* way home . . ."

"You don't care about comin' in anymore do you? You turning yeller like your friends at the academy? You told me once you liked what me and *my* friends did a lot more than them nose-grinders."

"Aw, c'mon, Ingo. Sure I like you. But I like Abner and Charlie, too. Any law against that?"

"Maybe you been listening too hard to the minister on Sabbath," Ingo muttered darkly.

181

"I'm goin' home . . ."

Ingo grabbed at Paul's sleeve, held him. "What I thought we'd do, well, it's something special —"

"All right. What?"

"Set fire to the teacher's house."

For a moment, Paul was too stunned for speech. Then he found his voice. *"Set fire to the nigger seminary?* Why, on a night like this, cold and windy, it'd burn clean to the ground in an hour!"

"That's exactly what I figgered."

"Ingo Lewis, I won't do any such thing! And you'd better not do it or I'll go straight to the sheriff. I rotten-egged, stoned, dumped garbage, and fouled wells at that place, and that's all I got stomach for. Why, setting a place on fire, the fanciest house in town, and right near Judsons' and Fenners' and not far from the church . . . what kind of an idea is that? You must be plumb addled."

"Oh well, I was just seein' what you'd say." Ingo laughed smoothly, reassuringly. "Matter 'fact, I never intended no such thing. I don't aim to be sent to no prison, though mad as Canterbury folk are they'd thank me for rousting the niggers out and finally sending 'em home. Paul, I never meant it at all. Still, can you keep a secret?"

"You know I can."

"Someone else is thinkin' of doin' it."

"Who?"

"Well, I can't say, not even to you, Paul. He's one of *them,* one like the brushy-haired gals."

"A *nigger* burn the seminary down?"

"That seminary's making it hard for niggers hereabouts. They don't *all* hold with such goings on."

"I can't think what nigger it could be. Had you better tell?"

"Naw. Nothing will come of it — this nigger's just full of talk. Besides, the less you and I and the rest of us boys tell the sheriff about the school, the better off we'll be. We done a pack of mischief around there and the sheriff just might think we'd fire it, too."

"I'm not going to ring the school bell, Ingo. I'm goin' home. And I'm not comin' in at night anymore." What part of Paul wasn't alarmed and disgusted felt immensely relieved. Ingo Lewis was scum. He'd known all along it was true. Ever since Ingo had dumped Paul off the horse, Paul's feelings had swung from the attraction of mischief to revulsion of the evildoer. Now with a thud his feelings settled down permanently. Paul didn't like the black school any more than ever, but he didn't like Ingo, either.

"Not goin' to ring an ole school bell? My, you *are* getting finicky . . ." Ingo's voice taunted.

"I'm not finicky; I'm just cold. I'll see you around, Ingo."

"Yeah, maybe you will," that hard voice said out of the darkness. "I always knew you was chicken livered and uppity . . ."

Several weeks later David brought home word of the school. The schoolgirls had wakened to the smell of smoke two days ago. That first day Prudence Crandall had searched her house from cellar to attic, room by room, even opening cupboards. She could find no fire anyplace, though the smell of smoke persisted. In such bitter weather David allowed as how the school must have gone to bed uneasily that night.

At nine o'clock this very morning, Sarah was coming up out of the basement when she glanced at a window and, horrified, saw a sheet of flame. She rushed upstairs, shouting alarm. Frantically Miss Crandall and the older girls cranked up water from the fouled well, ran around to the basement window and doused out the fire.

Going to another basement sill, Miss Crandall discovered how the fire had begun. Combustibles — bits of rag, kindling, odds and ends — had been tucked under corners where the basement window sills were decayed. In the winter dampness, and in the decayed wood, these combustibles had burnt like a slow match. But they finally ignited.

David was very careful to describe all this in detail. But the part he spoke about most fervently happened during the next few days.

Canterbury's Civil Authority called on Prudence Crandall. This delegation made no mention of danger to the schoolgirls. It said instead it was agitated to know the seminary nearly had been reduced to ashes, thus endangering the entire town.

"The Civil Authority says the culprit has been caught, a writ served on him, and his trial set," David reported. "The fire setter is the Negro clockmaker, Olney. But witnesses are required and the Civil Authority has served every member of Miss Crandall's school with a writ; every girl must attend Olney's trial in March. Maybe if Miss Crandall realizes she could burn down the town, she'll leave off," David finished grimly.

chapter 24

🌲🌲🌲🌲🌲🌲🌲🌲

IN MARCH, when the cock partridges drummed, and gold candles of new growth lit the tips of the pine branches, the fifth season, mud season, bogged everything down in a sucking brown sea.

Bernadette went out on the stoop for more kindling. In the farmyard Herod was tied to a post and Paul was currying his thick winter coat. The horse leaned in fierce contentment against the comb while balls of black fur blew here and there until they were finally trapped by the mud.

"Is Paul getting ready to take the horses somewhere?" Bernadette asked Hester.

"Yes, Bernadette, David is driving us all to Brooklyn for the Olney trial. Even Paul; Paul says he must go. For some reason he seems weighed down by the fire at the seminary." Bernadette hardly noticed Hester's mention of Paul.

Instead her heart leaped at the chance to see Miriam!

The buggy nearly foundered on the mucky trip over country lanes to the turnpike. On the safer six miles to Brooklyn, they passed a dozen neighbors and friends. Everyone waved and nodded — but solemnly — as though all were aware they were headed today for a portentous occasion.

How sick Prudence Crandall must be of the Brooklyn courthouse! Bernadette thought as the five of them squeezed into a crowded bench.

The Civil Authority of Canterbury — Judson, Bacon, Adams — congregated up front with a dozen weighty Canterbury citizens. The judge looked extraordinarily granite faced to Bernadette, but she was beginning to conclude all judges looked like that.

This time Miss Crandall sat down on the front bench with Almira and the Negro girls, about eighteen of them from old to young. Bernadette looked searchingly but couldn't find Miriam, no, nor Ann, nor Sarah. Where were the three older girls?

But what with wrestling the strong active baby, Bernadette had to give up wondering.

In the chair of the accused sat the slender, grizzle-haired Mr. Olney, one of the finest clockmakers in Connecticut. His eyes were downcast and his dark lined face was worried.

"He don't look so cheery," Paul whispered in Bernadette's ear. "I'd look scared too, if I'd done such a thing. *If* he did it . . ."

"Do you think he did it, Paul?"

"Well, that's what everyone says. Are those black girls really going to testify?"

"Some already have given testimony at other times. Miss Crandall never wanted them to testify before anyone because she said they'd had enough abuse, but finally Reverend May told Miss Crandall she should let the world see what good girls they were, not savages. Besides, they *have* to testify at this trial."

"I never heard a female speak up in public before." Paul's voice was awed.

"You'll hear one now."

If Prudence Crandall's second trial in the Indian summer

of October had been oven heated, it was no hotter than when Clockmaker Olney's trial commenced.

Most shocking of all was what the prosecution claimed. Its first witness declared Miss Prudence Crandall was tired of her school and had tried to burn it down!

"I'll be . . ." Paul exclaimed softly.

Bernadette couldn't believe her ears. But David ejaculated "amen" approvingly.

"That's not all," the Canterbury witness went on, swelling importantly. "The schoolmarm got the clockmaker to set the fire."

"Oh, thunder," Paul breathed.

Bernadette and Hester stared into each other's eyes. The ludicrous unreality of such a charge overwhelmed Bernadette.

"Did you ever hear such a thing?" Hester murmured.

"Will anyone believe it?" Bernadette whispered back, becoming aware of the rustlings around her. Excitement was ruffling the packed courtroom like puffs of wind across a ripe grain field. Sharp-eyed, attentive Judge Adams waved and poked his finger as the prosecution lawyers warmed to their charges. Several jurors looked wholeheartedly like they'd jump out of their jury box, fists raised.

Yes, Bernadette realized, people could take these charges seriously. A lot of people *wanted* to believe Miss Crandall would burn down her school, would set poor Olney to do it.

Claims and counterclaims bubbled and churned; in this legal cauldron the judge was having trouble keeping the lawyers in order. Everyone seemed to shout instead of talk.

Time passed.

Rachel clung to Bernadette, sucking her thumb with a rhythmic sound. Bernadette pulled the thumb away automatically. The baby, grunting, leaned over, trying to retrieve her comfortable pacifier. For a moment Bernadette's attention was focused on her tug-of-war with Rachel.

When she looked up, she realized there was a strange quiet in the room, a quiet like the one which precedes the tomcat's leap into the pigeon's nest.

Bernadette looked over her shoulder.

Here came Miriam! Miriam was walking up the aisle with Ann and Sarah.

As the black girls moved to the front of the room, Bernadette saw that Ann and Sarah walked with heads bowed and eyes downcast, but Miriam swung along negligently and even boldly appraised the crowd. David snorted.

A quiver ran down Bernadette's spine, a quiver which told her that with Miriam in an overexcited courtroom anything could happen.

As the three girls sat down, for the first time Miss Crandall stirred, nodding encouragement to her three students. Ann and Sarah smiled back but Miriam could best be said to have saluted.

The spectators rustled expectantly. At last they were going to get a chance to hear these black imps!

Bernadette pressed Rachel against her convulsively, then, when the baby wriggled protestingly, realized she was squeezing too tight. She felt like she was suffocating with waiting.

Finally, Ann's name was called. Ann rose, faced the room; in a soft voice she responded to the oath. She looked mortally frightened.

People strained forward to hear.

Ann told how she had come to the school, from where, and what she planned to do with her learning. She testified that Miss Crandall was the kindest and most devoted of teachers. Then, almost before the audience had taken it in, she was dismissed and sat down.

Well, that was one way to keep the pot from boiling over, Bernadette thought, praying the questions asked of Miriam — and what she replied to them — would be equally brief and noninciting.

Sarah was called to testify next. There were many in that room who knew Sarah and were better disposed toward her, for her family had lived around Canterbury since Connecticut slavery days. There was nothing abrasive in Sarah's manner, either; she was ladylike and chose her words carefully so as to give no offense.

Sarah said Miss Crandall would never have set her school on fire, would have been the last person in the world to get Mr. Olney in trouble. She described how the fire had been discovered and how the teachers and girls had put it out quickly and by themselves.

Miss Crandall's lawyer gave the schoolmarm a confident glance when Sarah sat down. Sarah had certainly offended no one.

He called Miriam's name next. Anxiety gripped Bernadette, for she sensed a vague, dissatisfied stirring in the audience as though it wanted a focus for its unfriendliness.

Miriam turned to face the courtroom. Memory came back in a flash to Bernadette, who remembered Miriam as she'd first looked in church and on the turnpike carrying the basket. Nobody but Bernadette knew it was the proud granddaughter of a princess of Timbo and a fighting Coromantee who surveyed these hostile villagers. But nobody had to guess that he was being looked down upon — it was all there in the line of Miriam's haughty, lifted head, the raking intensity of her glance. Just seeing her stand there, people would dislike her.

Irritation flashed unexpectedly in Bernadette. Just once — once when it was so desperately needed — couldn't Miriam be conciliatory?

It was clear the lawyer was unaware he had hold of a powder keg, because he began his questioning in a rapid, confident, oratorical style. But Miriam's first dry replies soon brought him up short, as his expression revealed in pained surprise.

"How did you get here?"

"I rode by stage from Providence to Brooklyn. It was an unpleasant ride," Miriam reported flatly.

"Why was that?" the lawyer asked.

"I was surrounded by blackguards who didn't know enough to be mannerly to strangers. But at Brooklyn I got away from the worst of them and walked to Canterbury. I liked the walk; the country here is far more beautiful than those who live in it . . ."

"Yes. Yes."

"When I arrived at Canterbury I was amazed to find the school was housed in the finest building on the green. Miss Crandall met me and helped me settle my things. She was kindness itself to me. From the beginning we've been well taught, better than most white girls — piano, drawing, painting, and even the French language. I liked the other schoolgirls and still do. They're gentle and defenseless and that makes it even harder for them to be brave. But they are, no matter how they're persecuted."

"What of the schoolteacher?" Hurriedly.

"Miss Crandall has been bravest of all. Though Canterbury folk" — how scornfully Miriam said it! — "have done everything to make her life miserable, she hasn't given up. Anyone who accuses Miss Crandall of setting our school afire has no notion of her. Besides, there isn't even any evidence against Mr. Olney . . . just a pack of lying gossip . . ."

David breathed hoarsely while Hester plucked at her skirt in agitation.

People were beginning to mutter. Bernadette could see heads together, hands cupped to ears, to lips. It seemed to her that a hot wind of hate would explode in that room at any minute. And who would its target be? Miriam!

"The school and the countryside are splendid," Miriam's voice went on inexorably. "All that is lacking is civilized people . . ."

All that is lacking is civilized people. The truth echoed in the air . . .

Rachel, forgive me, Bernadette breathed, and pinched the little arm. Waked from her slumber, the baby uttered a high, squalling scream. Hester jumped as though shot and Paul looked around, alarmed and flustered. The judge, the lawyers, the jury peered out into the room to see where the unseemly interruption came from. Even Miss Crandall glanced over her shoulder.

The baby's shrill, indignant wail kept up.

"What ails her?" Paul asked, red as a beet.

"I'll take her outside," Bernadette whispered to Hester.

191

She rose and stumbled over tight-packed feet, pressed against surprised knees, and finally came to the freedom of the aisle. She clattered up it and raced through the door.

Out on the steps she stood, shut her eyes, tried to catch her breath. She pressed Rachel to her, jiggling her, soothing her, her heart turning over for the pinched baby whom she loved.

But inside the courtroom, was it happening as she prayed it would?

A few minutes later Paul hunted her up as she waited with the baby in the shelter of a side doorway. She learned that she had provided the flustered lawyer with the time he needed to excuse his inconvenient witness.

"You may step down," Paul said the lawyer had commanded under cover of Rachel's commotion. Miriam had gone calmly back to her seat.

Bernadette leaned in the entry and pictured how the crowd must have blinked, coughed, wondered what had happened. But the moment of near riot had passed in the distraction of the crying child, the removal of the haughty Negro, the quick resumption of the defense's less inflammatory considerations. Without hostile focus, heightened feelings had subsided like water sucking away through sand.

A door banged. Ann, Sarah, and Miriam came out and headed toward Pardon Crandall's wagon.

Bernadette rushed to Miriam.

"Miss Crandall's lawyers say it won't take more than another hour for the case to be dismissed," Miriam informed. "They haven't a shred of evidence against either Miss Crandall or Mr. Olney."

"I'm so glad!" Bernadette breathed her relief. Then, "Will you go back to the school tonight?"

"No. Since we all had to come to Brooklyn, we're staying tonight at the Bensons' house; Miss Crandall is at the Mays'. We're going to have a party; we haven't had fun for such a long time. I wish you could stay with us and go home tomorrow."

They talked by the wagon another few minutes before Miriam had to leave. It was then Miriam told Bernadette to be on the lookout for a thin, balding, bespectacled, benign-faced man. It was hard to believe, but he was the famous fire-eating William Lloyd Garrison, who had come all the way to Brooklyn for this trial.

After they got home that night and the chores were done, Paul sat down near the hearth beside Bernadette and to her amazement asked for an extra needle. He picked up a shoe sole and began to work absently.

"I don't like the niggers, but there's never been anyone so relieved when the school didn't burn up," Paul sighed, jabbing the thong through the harsh leather. "And nobody *so* relieved when the nigger Olney got off. To tell the truth, I think Ingo Lewis did it. But I could never prove it."

And while Bernadette listened — half-amazed, yet confirmed in her worst suspicions — Paul confessed in a whisper what he and Ingo had done to the school, and finally told her what Ingo had suggested about the fire-setting.

Bernadette's feelings seethed in her. Twenty girls' lives risked! And the teacher's! And the town! And the suffering of Mr. Olney!

But thank heavens Paul had had nothing to do with a fire!

Paul put down the finished sandal and confided quietly, "I'm through with Ingo Lewis. Forever and ever."

193

"Oh, Paul, I hope you mean it!"

"You bet I mean it! I can't bear to look on him, he gives me such a sense of my own sinning. Of course Ingo'll make it hard for me. He's that sort."

"I'll stand with you." A totally new liking for Paul swept Bernadette. How glad she was to like him!

Paul's smile glowed soberly in the hearth fire and went clean to her heart.

"Thanks, Bernadette. But I'd best stand up for myself."

chapter 25

✝✝✝✝✝✝✝✝✝

Spring dripped and blew and finally bloomed into May. There was a sense of drift in the air. The church matter between Hester and David was unresolved; there was no solution as to where Bernadette could go, except to common school. Just as Bernadette couldn't drive herself back to the pointless hubbub of country school, Hester couldn't seem to go either to Quaker Meeting or back to the Canterbury church.

Finally Bernadette asked to go alone to Quaker Meeting. "I need to take Miriam's books back to her." David consented grudgingly.

At Meeting, Miriam told Bernadette Miss Crandall had gone to Boston in April and had had her portrait painted. Letters were coming to her from all over the country, even from England and Scotland. "But winter was like living inside a box." Miriam sighed. "Winter and enmity both closed us in. So often I longed to run to North Hill to talk to you. You don't have to give back the books. I can borrow Ann's."

"I've memorized all three of them," Bernadette answered quietly.

When Bernadette trudged into the orchard, Hester was waiting for her. "I'm not going to Black Hill anymore, Bernadette," Hester explained somberly. "I decided this morning. All winter I've prayed. My prayers have finally told me maybe I can do more among enemies than friends. I'm going to work at the Canterbury church. I'm going to help Prudence Crandall by trying to start a female antislavery society. Yes, right in the village."

So all of them went back to church, Paul beaming, David gratified, Hester determined, Rachel entranced with wagon riding, Bernadette with long memories of the first time she had heard the shrill minister and seen the black girls suffer in that church.

But the old easiness between Hester and David returned at last.

With renewed tenacity, when summer began, Bernadette drove herself back to the dusty hot common school, listlessly swinging her tied-up primers.

Time was passing quickly for Bernadette. The institute in the forest and Pastor Fry seemed worlds away. What kept her dream from dimming into extinction was one thing: Miriam. Miriam, who had begun again to come faithfully to meet her on the heights of North Hill.

Paul decided he needed Bernadette. He had to teach the newborn calf to drink from a bucket. Sabbath or not, it couldn't wait any longer to be taken from its mother.

Paul got up, brushed the straw from his pantaloons, went out of the barn.

He threw open the kitchen door and called for Bernadette. Far away her voice answered. In a minute there she was, knowing already what he wanted. They walked silently together across the farmyard.

"It's nursed three days now," Paul commented. "Pa says we got to start it to drink by itself today."

The barn was shadowed and hospitable; in some ways barns were nicer than houses, Paul thought.

The cow looked around at them with her sad brown eyes; beside her, the little calf stood trustingly on brave skinny legs. They got the calf shooed away from its mother and out into an empty stall. They wouldn't dare wean a calf with the mother close enough to kick.

After Bernadette fetched the pail, Paul poured the skim milk — set aside for the first lesson — into it.

"I'll hold the calf," Paul instructed, "and you poke your finger in its mouth. If *I* try to lean over and poke mine in, I always just poke the eye."

"Hold the calf tight and I'll help push its head in the pail," Bernadette offered.

They both chased the small brown captive into a corner. Paul anchored the calf's hind end against a wall, then straddled it, and pressed tight against the strong protesting body.

It was embarrassing how he'd had to explain to Bernadette the finger in the calf's mouth made it think it had hold of a tit and what with sucking on the finger, if its head was held down to the skim-milk pail, it would surprise itself and drink. But he was amazed how cool Bernadette had been about it; only said she understood, and then, with the other calf, had done such a good job it had learned to drink in no time flat. She seemed to have a way with animals. Babies, too. She'd make a good farmer's wife someday.

Yet with his squeezing and Bernadette's pushing, they still couldn't get this calf's head right over the pail. It kept squirming and backing off. Finally they got it pulled into

197

position, Paul pressed his legs with all his might, and pushed on the head. Bernadette, on her hands and knees, had her finger shoved in the calf's mouth and with the other hand was helping to drag the head into the milk when the calf made a choking sound, its head flew up, and sure enough, it did what Paul hated worst of all — it blew milk all over the place, even backward so it pelted him. It fairly drenched his kneeling companion.

Bernadette rocked back and peals of laughter shook her as she mopped at her wet face and dress. Paul was thinking what an unusual girl she was — most were so almighty persnickety about clothes — when a voice spoke right over his shoulder and nearly knocked him flat with surprise.

"You goin' to drown the calf or it goin' to drown you?" drawled the voice. The hair crawled on the back of Paul's neck but he didn't turn his head.

"What are you doing here, Ingo?" he asked, painfully casual.

"Just came up to see where you've been all these months," the voice replied slickly.

"School, and besides there's been spring plowing . . ."

"Someone else's had our fun at the nigger school. Set that fire in January but the sills were so rotted it wouldn't blaze. Olney said he didn't do it, but niggers all lie . . ."

Bernadette, still on her heels, stared hard up into Ingo's face. "It was a terrible thing to do! What if someone had been killed?"

"What if?" Ingo countered, his voice slippery as butter.

Paul didn't dare look at Ingo, only pretended to be getting a better grip on the calf, who didn't need it now and was standing amazed. But he had a full view of Bernadette's indignant face, brown eyed, apple red, and so pretty when she was excited or mad. With a kind of agony Paul watched Bernadette's anger as she glared up at Ingo. Paul wanted to shout to Bernadette to get up and run, if she could still skin through the stall entrance. She didn't know what meanness there was in Ingo. Instead she kept on talking.

"I'll bet you set that fire! Nobody but the worst person alive would set fire to a schoolhouse in the dead of a winter night."

"So Paul been talking to you," Ingo answered. There was something sleepy in his voice, sleepy, crawly. And the voice was coming closer to the stall, Paul realized. Where was everyone? With a sickening sensation, Paul remembered his father had gone down to patch up the rock in the lower pasture wall where the sheep were grazing.

"You *are* hateful." Bernadette blazed. But now she got up and her eyes began to open in a strange, wary way, and there was Ingo at Paul's elbow, only too far off to reach, and then he was edging past him, getting closer to Bernadette. Paul nudged the calf; it kicked and bucked.

"Ingo, we got a chore to do." Paul spoke sharply. "You better wait outside the stall till we get finished . . ."

"Maybe I better," Ingo said, never even turning his head. "And then again maybe I better not."

"You wait outside!" Paul shouted in sudden fury.

"*You* wait outside," Ingo answered.

Paul leaped off the calf, kicked at it to get it out of his road, and landed on Ingo's broad back, his arms going round the boy's neck and jerking him backward onto the straw. Ingo would lick him, lick the stuffing out of him. But there was no help for it.

200

"Run!" he shouted to Bernadette and then he didn't think of her anymore because Ingo had twisted around and was on his hands and knees heading for him. Paul was pinned by arms far stronger than his own; he was trying not to feel the first pain of Ingo's pummeling.

Bernadette tangled with the wobbly calf, righted herself and leaped for the stall entrance. Frantically she raced toward the open barn door where she ran smack into David.

"Bernadette! What's wrong?"

"They're having a fight," she breathed. Instantly David ran after her, hearing as she did the scraping on the barn floor, the muffled thumps and grunts.

David encountered the stunned calf, too, but it wasn't a split second before he flattened it against the wall and waded into the fight, his arms flailing. He dragged the two boys up from the tangled heap on the floor.

"Stop this! Stop! It's the Sabbath!" David roared.

But powerful as he was, he was no match for the twisting Ingo. Before he could get a new grip, Ingo tore himself out of David's grasp, streaked past the startled Bernadette, and thudded out of the barn.

"Now what is the meaning of this?" David furiously demanded of his son. "What's that rapscallion doing here?"

"If you please," Paul said, straw sticking to his hair and one eye swelling up, "I'd like to speak with you, Father. I've got a lot of things I have to confess."

Paul unburdened everything. Egg and rock throwing, refuse dumping, well fouling. After the broil of it, after Hester's shamed weeping, David's shouting, and Paul's stoical

punishment, it was as if the guilt of it shocked David's mind into a new path.

He said soberly, "Though with all my heart I wish it weren't so, perhaps the school *is* here to stay. That means, Wife, we must really decide what we can do for Bernadette."

chapter 26

†††††††††

P_{AUL} LEFT Fenner's Store and went out into a soft June mist. He'd delivered his mother's butter and eggs and collected her coins, and if it had only been brighter, he'd have really taken his time riding home.

He exchanged greetings with a pair of loafers — rain or shine, there was always someone spitting and jawing on Fenner's steps — and headed across the road to his wagon.

The side door of the black school opened and Paul saw a man come out. He recognized him as young Mr. Burleigh, who helped teach the brushy-haired girls. Paul hadn't seen him very often so he leaned on the other side of Sheba and peered curiously around the horse's nose at the fellow.

Slender, erect, not bad-looking. Sober as a deacon but dressed natty and regular, with nicely-trimmed brown hair. The young teacher cut across the side lawn and went down the slope to the Plainfield Road.

"Hey, you there!"

Paul jumped at the sudden derisive catcall.

"Nigger lover!"

The teacher never looked to right nor left, just strode faster.

Paul squinted down the road and saw at once where the taunts came from. Ingo Lewis and Charlie Long were leaning against a tree trunk at the end of the seminary lot.

"Where you goin'?" Charlie bawled. "All dressed so pretty . . ."

As he said it, Charlie raised his arm and threw, and there was a *plop* as the well-aimed egg struck the young teacher square on the head.

Mr. Burleigh stopped and swerved around to face his tormentors.

And was instantly caught by a hail of rotten eggs.

The boys must have loaded up, been laying in wait. Paul whistled to himself. Eggs dripped from the teacher's shoulder, sleeve, coat frock, leg. And one even dripped down that well-cut hair. My, but he must smell!

"C'mon, fight; see if you dare!"

"He wouldn't fight, not him." Paul heard Ingo guffaw. "What you expect from a feller who learns niggers to play the py-ano?"

Would the young teacher fight? Paul wondered intently.

Mr. Burleigh glared at Ingo and Charlie, pulled out his handkerchief, mopped his hair and forehead, then spun on his boot heel and stalked back up the bank to the seminary.

"Look at him turn tail!"

The rest of the eggs made an odiferous ruin of the back of the teacher's nice suit.

Paul was now aware that people were watching, amused, from Fenner's Store, that children gawked from lawns and porches, that up the road dashed a couple of latecomer boys eager to join the tormenting.

Paul hurtled himself up into the wagon the minute the seminary door slammed shut on Mr. Burleigh.

He was surprised to find himself fuming. He was ashamed at what he'd done at the school, would never molest it again, nor did he believe others should damage it — instead, wear it out by cold-shouldering. But he wasn't ashamed he misliked the brushy-haired girls or the pig-headed schoolmarm who didn't give a rap how she tore the village apart.

No, he was fuming for the young teacher instead. Ingo and Charlie had picked on a white man, a regular-looking fellow. To Paul that was somehow different, there was something unforgivable in that.

Why hadn't the teacher fought Ingo and Charlie? he asked himself grimly as he bounced down the lane toward home. Well, he couldn't blame Mr. Burleigh for avoiding that. Paul knew all too well what it was like to take Ingo's pummeling.

As soon as he got home, he hunted up Bernadette and described what had happened. She listened with her usual intensity; she was one girl who listened as hard as she talked. Her eyes said she was heartsick, disgusted; then they snapped.

It came to Paul, looking into those expressive brown eyes, those sometimes sparkling, sometimes pensive, often determined brown eyes, that he should have taken the teacher's part, gone to Mr. Burleigh's rescue.

All day while he worked in the haymow, Paul thought about what he should have done. In his mind he pictured all kinds of different dramatic rescues he could have led.

He'd like to have helped out the teacher. But better than that, he'd liked to have been a hero to Bernadette.

Sympathizer for Mr. Burleigh or not, Paul was as sour and impatient as any villager when, on July 22, the high court quashed the third case against Prudence Crandall, claiming the state of Connecticut hadn't presented adequate legal evidence. The contest seemed ended; Miss Crandall had won for good. In the heat of the summer noon, the village lay torpid and stunned. Folk whispered in little knots at the general store, their expressions saying they couldn't believe Miss Crandall had beaten them. No church bells were rung, no triumphant drums rolled, no horns blared, and no exultant cannons were shot. An ominous quiet settled over Canterbury.

The decision of the court satisfied Bernadette. At last she'd reconciled herself that she must find some other school — somewhere, somehow, sometime. That she would eventually find a school, she never once doubted now. If she had to earn her own way at Oberlin as a grown woman after years of working, she'd get there.

But now she was fiercely glad for Miss Crandall, fiercely glad for Miriam and the school. So was Hester glad, though in front of glum David and Paul, both celebrated by the discreet communion of understanding looks.

Not long afterward, more exciting news came, news Bernadette and Hester felt free to talk about openly.

"Guess what the tinker told me this forenoon, David!" Hester exclaimed at suppertime as she started to ladle.

"What gossip is that, Wife?" David asked amiably, tucking his napkin into his collar.

"He said Miss Crandall was wed."

"Miss Crandall," David repeated absently, then he caught on. *"Miss Crandall! The schoolmarm?"*

207

"Some man really married *her?*" Paul asked, thunder-struck, spoon halfway to mouth.

"Why, of course. She's a fine woman, Paul."

Paul's face registered vast skepticism; the teacher didn't have the air of a marrying woman, his look said.

"When did this happen?" David inquired carefully.

"The tinker was putting away his mending tools when he thought to tell me," Hester replied. "Said the couple had kept their marriage plans mighty quiet. It seems they went to Packerville to be wed just yesterday."

"Well," David broke in impatiently, "who did she wed?"

"Mr. Philleo," Bernadette told him. "He's a preacher from Ithaca, New York. He's big and has red hair. He was at Miss Crandall's last trial."

"I believe I did hear some chap like that was hanging about," David observed. "Older than the schoolmarm, isn't he? Widower with a half-grown daughter. A Baptist, Fenner said."

"Baptist," Paul speculated. "They shout a lot, don't they, Pa? Maybe a shouting fellow like that won't stand for a mule-headed wife, will make her give up her school."

"On the other hand," Hester retorted, "Miss Crandall's marrying a strong man might just transform the school from temporary into permanent. I'm glad for the teacher, any-way, however the school turns out. She's had enough ter-rible trouble."

"What else did the tinker say?" David asked, spearing a potato.

"He said Miss Crandall went with her sister Almira over to Packerville. Later the wedding party came back in chaises and carts to the school. The teacher wore a white shawl and carried a Bible . . ."

"That tinker knows everything." David snorted. "And tells it. Well, where are the blissful couple now?"

"He said Mr. Philleo moved into the school yesterday," Bernadette answered.

"Pa, do you think it will make any difference?" Paul asked insistently.

"I don't know, Paul." His father sighed. "I'm too worn down to guess."

chapter 27

✝✝✝✝✝✝✝✝

Digging potatoes was dirty, hot work. When midafternoon came and she and Paul had gone endlessly up and down the rows, Bernadette wasn't surprised to hear Paul declare suddenly, "We've got these early ones most dug. Pa's out to the orchard with Neighbor Shaw, so I'm going down to the stream."

Bernadette chopped the ground silently. What would it feel like to put her dusty bare feet in cool stream water? Being a girl she'd never know.

"You want to come, too?" Paul asked impulsively.

He couldn't mean it. "Aunt Hester will need me for the supper getting."

"Not for an hour. We'll be back quicker than that."

Bernadette looked down at the brown mounds of potatoes, up at the cobalt-hot September sky, down again to her draggled skirt hem and dirty feet with their burning soles. Suddenly she threw down her hoe. Without a word she skimmed across the ground, Paul running after her in amazement. He was puffing by the time they got to the plank bridge.

Beyond the bridge, Bernadette slid down the bank and plopped her scorched feet right in the lovely water. Paul stared a minute at her blissful face, its eyes closed, then disappeared into the bushes. But he came back with a sheepish look, for he'd suddenly realized if he was going to swim he'd have to go in with his clothes on. Well, that was better than not being cool at all. He splashed in with a shout, plunged forward into the deep swimming hole. Then he turned over on his back and floated. He watched Bernadette sitting down by the bridge bank cooling her tired feet, studying the minnows and water bugs.

"Be nice if you could swim," he shouted.

She looked up and shook her head.

"You can wade right there in front of you up to your arms. Go ahead. We'll sit in the sun and dry out before we go home."

Could she? Bernadette asked herself, trying to imagine what it would feel like to be wet and dripping all over. Would her petticoats dry in time?

She musn't. But oh, she had been good for so long! Good with the constant, gripping goodness required of any-one taken in charity under a stranger's roof. For two years she had watched everything she did or said so the Frys wouldn't mind her living with them.

A wanton madness overtook her. She skidded from the bank right into the water, bumping her panteletted bottom when she landed on a flat stone. She sat there, stunned by the cool water, stunned by the sight of her legs floating out in front of her, white and wavy.

The she laughed; she thought she'd never stop laughing.

"What's the matter?" Paul shouted, alarmed.

"Nothing," she reassured him. "It just feels so good."

"Don't it though?" he agreed fervidly and turned over on his belly to propel himself through the water with exuberant strokes. He wished Bernadette could swim out there with

211

him. But girls couldn't, of course. They were too fragile and it was too hard with all that skirt stuff wrapped around them. Yet suddenly he wondered if Bernadette *could* learn to swim. She'd be the plucky kind who'd love swimming.

He kicked back across the deep pool and stood up, dripping, not far from where she sat.

"You like to learn how?" he asked.

Her eyes shone instantly with that wistful look he noticed more often. Funny how there were so many appealing things he hadn't noticed before.

"But I couldn't."

"You be scared to try? I could hold you up."

She looked dubiously at the deep pool, black and still under the shadow of the willows.

"It ain't hard," Paul encouraged. "I learned fast. You lay on the water and kick your feet and make your arms go."

She kept on looking undecided.

"Come on, try! Stand here on the rocks at the edge of the hole, then when I get my arm under you, lay out headfirst on the water. I won't let you sink."

Suddenly she stumbled up and before he knew what she was doing, she lay right out on the deep water as he'd told her to. He made a rush for her, grabbed a handful of her clothes at the waist, then got his arms under her. Though she kicked like a regular windmill, it was harder than he'd thought. He was losing his footing as she nudged him out into the deep water.

They struggled and thrashed.

Paul wasn't sure what moment he'd first heard the voices. They'd probably been far-off and unnoticed, lost in the noise of Bernadette's valiant churning.

213

When he did hear them, they weren't far away.

He pulled Bernadette roughly through the water. Her face went under and she came up spluttering, rubbing her eyes.

"That's Ingo," Paul whispered. She turned and looked over her shoulder and he'd not forget the look in her eye.

"Hurry!" he murmured, pushing and pulling her over the rocks. They splashed up the high bank together.

"Hide!" he ordered as they scrambled toward the bushes.

They collapsed inside the woodsy screen and huddled, drippy and sticking together, not able to see, but well able to hear.

"Listen!" he hissed. "It's George and Tim and Ingo come swimming. They'll spend most of their time down beyond us."

The boys passed dangerously close and Bernadette wondered how long you could hold your breath without dying. Paul wriggled around in the bushes so he could peer out. After a bit, he tunneled on through the undergrowth, motioning for her to stay behind. She could see the sunny brightness of the hole he made for himself at the bank's edge.

They were going swimming all right, Paul saw. Tim was already in the water, his head bobbing. Suddenly, like a comet, Ingo erupted from under the willows and ran for the pool, plummeting in feet first, nose held. Howling like an Indian, George followed.

Paul clutched at his leafy peephole with a convulsed hand. There were two things he must do for Bernadette if it took every ounce of manhood in him. First, he had to keep her hidden from Ingo. Second, he had to keep her from seeing out to the swimming hole. Three heaps of pantaloons and shirts lay on the bank.

He slithered quickly back to her. "You stay here," he ordered fiercely. "I'll stay up there so's to keep everyone in sight. But don't you dare come with me."

"I don't have to see them; I can hear them. That's enough," Bernadette retorted.

Crouched in the underbush, everything muddy and steamy around her, she counted the dragging minutes. All she could see now of Paul were the dirty soles of his feet and his pantaloon legs. His toes wiggled distractedly.

She couldn't stay blank with fear forever. After a while, she recited the catechism. She declined Latin. Finally, she began to ask herself questions from Miriam's books, discovering she'd forgot very little of them. She slid around to another spot because her old one was gluey. Her hair was beginning to dry.

All at once, she saw Paul's toes grow still; his legs stiffened ominously. As she listened intently, voices came toward them. Someone was swimming down toward the shallow creek. They were splashing right below the bank where they lay and their voices rose up, every word clear as an anvil.

"Pa says tonight is the night, George." It was Ingo's voice. "He and some of the men are going to batter down the doors and really wreck that old school. Pa don't know I'm goin' to be there but you can bet I wouldn't miss that much fun for anything."

"What time?" George's voice asked.

"Midnight."

"They going to do anything else but wreck? Fire, or anything?"

"I don't know. Could be. I know I'm going to scare those nigger girls so they'll jump clean out the upstairs windows."

"But Ingo, the teacher has a husband now."

"So she has a husband," Ingo's voice replied scornfully. "He'll be too busy wringing his hands. Who'd marry a dragon like that? Some old granny in breeches, for sure."

"I heard he was a blacksmith before he was a parson. Tim says he seen him and he's a big, strong-looking fellow."

"So who cares? I don't aim to walk right up to him and let him grab me. It's goin' to be dark and everyone excited."

There was low murmuring. Finally Ingo and George must have swum away because in a minute they were yelling down at the pool.

They were going to wreck the school! The words went around and around in Bernadette's shocked mind, trapped there.

She wouldn't believe it. She couldn't believe it.

She knew with a great despair it was true.

She threw a dirt clod at Paul's bare foot. He inched back toward her, his eyes big and questioning.

"Did you hear what Ingo said?" she whispered fiercely.

"Of course. You think I was asleep?"

"Do you believe him?"

"Nah. There's been a lot of plans like this one and half never got done."

"I'm going home," Bernadette announced to Paul. She didn't know what home could do for her; but she couldn't sit still another minute and think about the school and the teacher and Miriam Hosking.

Paul grabbed her arm. "Don't you stir!" he hissed. "They're ready to quit. Then we can light out."

She crouched back under cover and prayed, eyes shut, the boys would go quickly. *Go away. Go away,* her mind chanted.

Our gracious Lord replied. With rowdy hooting and hallooing, the boys climbed up the bank. Their voices were a bad dream as they passed near their hiding place. Then words blurred and finally distance extinguished them.

Paul burst out of the bushes and squatted beside her.

"Whoo!" he said. "I'd hate to go through that waiting another time."

"Paul, we have to tell someone about the school."

He didn't answer, only pulled her up, scrambling ahead of her through the brush. At the plank bridge they looked around carefully. No one was in sight. Then they half walked, half ran up the country road.

"Paul, we have to tell someone about the school," she repeated, stopping.

This time he couldn't ignore her. "Oh, I don't think anything'll come of all that talk," he answered uneasily. "Ingo's a terrible braggart."

"He said it was going to happen."

"Well, what should we do?" Paul suddenly cried. "If I tell Pa I took you swimming all by yourself and Ingo came by, he'll thrash me to an inch of my life. And Ma won't like your getting your clothes all wet and being so unladyfied."

"I don't care," Bernadette replied stubbornly. "I'm going to tell Aunt Hester anyway."

"Now look, Bernadette, don't say a word to anyone when we get home. I'll take care of warning the school tonight, I promise I will."

He'd climbed down the tamarack tree by his window a lot

of times for thoroughly bad reasons. But he'd confessed and turned over a new leaf. Even if he still didn't care for the black girls, Bernadette knew she could trust Paul now.

"You promise?" She wouldn't budge, waiting for his answer.

"I promise! Now come on. We've got to run up and down in the sun to dry out our clothes. Let's hope Ma thinks the mud was from the potato digging."

Hester looked sharp at Bernadette for being late to help with the meal because Rachel was underfoot and the milk sauce for the salt codfish had scorched in the pot.

Sitting on the back stoop in the late-summer twilight, Bernadette sewed on a slave sandal. She pulled the thong distractedly as Miriam's face floated out of the shadows. Miriam's eyes smiled with no contention in them; she stretched, lazy and humorous, under the North Hill tree. Other recollections swam before Bernadette: Miriam was running up the pike with the boys hot behind her; Miriam lay battered in the candlelight and spoke secretly to Bernadette; far below Miriam rode in the wagon down the dusty Black Hill Road.

Bernadette went up to her room early, lay nervously on the bed, the window open beside her, and stared out into the deepening night. She listened for the rest of the family to come up. Finally she listened for Paul to crawl, rustling and grunting, into the tree.

She wasn't sleepy; her body felt hurtfully tense.

It was hard to tell how fast time passed, but she thought it grew alarmingly late. And still she heard nothing — not the faintest sign of life from Paul's room. Probably, without meaning to, Paul had fallen asleep.

218

She'd have to go to the village herself.

She got up and moved softly across the boards in her bare feet, found her clothes on the chair in the corner, pulled on her undergarments, petticoat and dress, recoiling from the stiff, muddy skirt. She couldn't risk the noise of shoes — barefoot she'd be silent as a cat. She picked up her little Bible from the top of the chest, the pair of slave sandals she had just finished. She opened her door and crept downstairs, glad she had long ago discovered which steps creaked.

The kitchen door, once the bolt was carefully slipped, made a fearful *chirk* she was sure would wake the dead. She waited, heart pounding. But only silence met her anguished pause.

She peered out into the dark. She hadn't realized how deep it could be.

If she hesitated any longer before that black wall, she'd never have the courage to pierce it. She went down the steps and skimmed across the familiar farmyard, came to the tree-hung country lane. She stopped and pushed her feet into the oversized slave slippers. Then she drew a last deep breath and plunged into velvet shade.

Not being able to see made the sounds twice as loud: the croak of the frogs at the swimming hole, the thump of her running feet on the plank bridge, the rustle of leaves, and once the sudden explosion of a deer across her path. After the deer, she had to stop till her knees steadied again.

But at least no bobcats screamed from those dark trees the way they had that night coming home from Oberlin with Pastor Fry.

Where was Ingo Lewis right now? Fear engulfed her. She ran on.

219

She scrambled up to the pike. She'd meant to run straight up the highway because it would be smoother in the dark, but in the open she felt suddenly exposed and vulnerable. So she shot down into the underbrush again, not cutting cross-lots, but clinging to the stone walls and skirting the brushy, too-shadowed places.

Would she be at the school before the wreckers? Would she meet them someplace? she wondered frantically.

She collided with a rock, stumbled, fell headlong to the rough ground. For a second she clung there, clung to the safety of the earth, wanting to burrow into it, wanting to escape the dangers which hovered above. But she picked herself up, limped briefly, began to hurry as soon as she could.

She slipped under the gate at the bridge — Ingo Lewis country. She raced over the bridge without notice. Out of the blind blackness, orderly shapes began to loom up — the roof lines of the village houses. She was nearly there.

Her relief was short-lived. If there were men, they might be hiding around her. She stopped, wishing she had feelers like a bug. She listened, her ears bursting with effort. Nothing — no sounds except peaceful nighttime ones.

Bernadette made swiftly for Miss Crandall's distinctive roof line. It was unthinkable to go up to the front door and rap loudly on it, so she eased into the big side yard. Was the Bible still in her hand? Somehow, she still clung to it.

She knew Miriam's window because there was a tamarack tree by it. It wasn't the best tree for climbing, but she managed to pull herself into its lower branches and looked up at that window. Again the Lord was merciful. Miss Crandall frowned on window opening, but Miriam was a rebel and her window was half-raised. Bernadette propped her trembling body against the tamarack trunk and hurled the little book as hard as she could. She heard it thud when it landed on the floor inside.

A dark head thrust out.

"Get Miriam!" she called, low and urgent.

"I'm Miriam. Who's there?"

"It's Bernadette."

"What . . ."

"Let me in the house."

"Come to the ell door," Miriam instructed.

Bernadette jumped out of the tree, leaving a strip of torn skirt behind.

She waited on the door stoop, satisfaction beginning to take the place of gripping fear. She'd gotten to the school in time!

Suddenly, at the front of the house she heard the murmur of a man's deep voice. Bernadette dropped in a heap and huddled up flat to the door. *Miriam, come!* she implored.

The door opened a crack and Bernadette rolled inside in a heap. Miriam stooped over, shaking her shoulder — Miriam, who had wisely brought no light.

"Bar the door," Bernadette breathed.

"I did. What is it? Are you all right?"

"Men are coming to wreck the school!" Even as Bernadette spoke there was a sound like the crack of doom — glass breaking in the front of the house.

Abruptly Bernadette was on her feet following with stumbling steps Miriam's headlong flight up strange stairs.

On the floor above, they shot past closed doors from behind which came a first stirring of sleepy voices.

221

They burst into Miriam's room. Bernadette could see heads raised up from white pillows. One of Miriam's younger roommates was beginning a soft wail.

"Get under the bed!" Miriam ordered Bernadette. Bernadette rolled into the boxlike darkness, stunned.

"But why?" she protested, thrusting her head out from under the counterpane, desperately trying to locate Miriam.

Miriam stooped down beside her. "If the school's broken into, they'll find you. Now, hush!" the Negro implored savagely. Bernadette's head was roughly crammed back into its hiding place.

The bedroom door opened and a voice spoke out of the shadows. It was the voice of the teacher. "Miriam, you're in charge of the girls in this room. Keep the small ones comforted. Mr. Philleo and I will be in the hall if you need us. Pray, dear girls, pray for the Lord's protection." It was a small voice, yet clear and steady.

While Prudence Crandall Philleo held the door open, Bernadette counted two more windows broken, then a third. The sound tore at her as though through her flesh.

The teacher closed the door and left; noises grew harder to distinguish. Yet no closed door could obliterate the thudding and thumping, the heavy, hard-toned voices below. Bernadette poked her head out and saw Miriam outlined in the window's faint glow, a cluster of white-robed girls crowding around her. Miriam rocked back and forth crooning, "There, there, there," like the tick of a clock. The other girls whispered together; one sobbed.

The most terrible convulsion burst forth. The whole house shook with concussions, concussions made by what must be iron bars and heavy clubs fracturing tables, splintering chairs, cracking mirrors and pictures, shattering lamps, dismembering students' desks, senselessly thumping on walls and floors.

Would there be anything left at all? Bernadette asked herself numbly.

Another window sash torn, another window shattered. One of the girls bawled in terror.

This time when the bedroom door opened, it was a man's voice which spoke. "Young ladies," it said, "get on your knees; let us pray." Girls scrambled to the floor; a flash of hysterical amusement swept over Bernadette because she was already trapped on her knees.

"Our Father in heaven . . ." Prudence Crandall's new husband began, then was interrupted by a terrified girl's voice from out in the hall. He never got past that "Our Father in heaven." He rushed away.

If that was Mr. Philleo, he's more distraught than the schoolmarm, Bernadette concluded sadly. Where was Miss Crandall's strong shoulder to lean upon?

Miriam's face suddenly peered in at her. It was a God-given moment. Bernadette had something she'd been wanting to tell Miriam.

"There's a village boy named Ingo," she whispered. "He might come upstairs."

The Negro girl's voice was hard. "I know about him," she replied. "Sarah heard him brag one day."

"Miriam, what should we do if . . ."

"You just do as I say. No braggart is going to come in here." Miriam disappeared before Bernadette could argue about coming out from under the bed to help in their defense.

223

The black girl went to the door and opened it a crack. The schoolmarm and her husband were speaking in the hall.

"But what if they set a fire?" the man's voice exclaimed. There was a cautioning "Shhh!" Then the teacher's dim form reentered their room; girls crowded around her. Bernadette pulled in her head.

"Be brave," the teacher spoke. From below came an especially great thud, a raucous shout.

Prudence Crandall Philleo sat down for a moment on the edge of the bed Bernadette hid under, sat and said nothing. While she was there Bernadette had the impression that she was shaking silently. Was her trembling from passionate anger or helpless fear?

But when she got up her voice was controlled. "I'll be back soon," and she left.

"Don't cry, don't cry," Miriam crooned.

What could possibly be left to wreck downstairs?

That meant they'd soon come upstairs to wreck. Where was Ingo Lewis? Bernadette asked herself.

The pandemonium below had begun with a shocking abruptness.

More chilling still was the quickness with which it stopped.

Bernadette's stunned ears adjusted disbelievingly from loudness to silence. In the room a girl hiccoughed noisily. The rest waited, utterly still.

Fire, the husband had warned. Bernadette sniffed, sniffed again. There was a rustling at the closed door. Bernadette thought of Ingo in the silence. She ached from waiting.

Minutes moved by, slow, crawling minutes . . .

Then there were voices again in the hall, one raised angrily in words which Bernadette never forgot: "My dear," Mr. Philleo was saying, "we can't go on like this. The girls must be sent away tomorrow." There was a woman's murmured protest. A door closed. The awesome silence once more.

"Bernadette! Bernadette Savard."

Where did that harsh whisper come from? she wondered, terrified.

Unthinkingly, Bernadette jerked her head up; it collided with the frame of the bed and she nearly fainted. But when the dizzy spell passed, Miriam was there. And there beside her, of all people, was Paul Fry. "I fell asleep," Paul whispered. "I'm sorry, I'm terrible sorry, Bernadette."

Hands pulled her from her hiding place and she was floating on strange, unreal feet as she fled into the upper back hall, Miriam leading her, Paul stumbling along behind. She noted the rising, confused babble of voices from the bedrooms, and as they descended to the darkness below, she saw above the leap of a candle flame.

The three of them passed into the morning room. There was no way to see the destruction, but it was felt: plaster crunching underfoot, rubbled dust pulsating in the dim air. The door hung crazily open. Miriam crossed the doorsill with her, then let go of her.

"Good-bye." The black girl's voice sounded breathy and dreamlike to Bernadette.

With Paul's hand clasped where Miriam's had let go, Bernadette leaped into a vast dark sea of grass.

Tomorrow Miriam Hosking would journey home, out of her life.

225

chapter 28

✝✝✝✝✝✝✝✝

Next day, Bernadette learned Reverend May had hurried from Brooklyn to the school, and on his advice, the black students had been sent home. Reverend Philleo offered a reward of fifty dollars for the apprehension of the ruffians responsible for the destruction. Impenetrable silence and sidelong glances were all that met his efforts at justice.

He closed his wife's school.

"Of course, why not?" David asked at the table. "Who wants to go to the expense of repair since there'd be no assurance the attack wouldn't be repeated? It's clear no one in town will protect the school." He applauded the superior wisdom of Reverend Philleo. But — apparently not unmindful of Hester's stricken look — he told his wife she might take *The Liberator* again. He said he himself might look into this new antislave society.

To Bernadette it seemed as though David Fry dared turn critical of faraway Southern slave owners only now that the Negroes were swept from his own doorstep.

Judging by the letter which came to Bernadette a few weeks later, Pastor Fry was riddled with the same conflicts; Pastor, who wanted the blacks to be free but was uncomfortable when they were close.

. . . my brother David writes me the black school has gone down and possibly it will be just a matter of time before the village can find a good schoolmistress to reopen the seminary on its old white basis — David and Hester would like you to stay with them — If you choose to stay there, I'm glad the school has gone down for, partisan as I'm growing to the cause of the slave and close as you feel to the girls at the school, I still can't think of your living among blacks and being educated with them — Judging by your impassioned letters in defense of your Miriam and the black girls, you and I have much to talk about — Another possibility for your schooling is close to my heart, Aunt Leah having finally agreed to give up your help — If you don't stay at Canterbury, come home to us, dear little Bernadette — I've inquired at Oberlin and they tell me they would accept you for the preparatory course if you and I studied together diligently — Naturally, if the Canterbury school develops, it will offer you more advantages, but what I can offer is a certainty, not just a possibility — plus warm welcome back! Besides, dashing young Jonathan commands you to come before he must go to Yale — He wants two more years to tease you and pull your braids and romp with you in the fields before you must, in God's own time, grow up . . .

She walked up the road into the village. Straight ahead the graceful seminary loomed behind its white fence. It was all she could see.

She opened the gate, clicked it shut, stood — hands in

apron pockets — and looked up. The beautiful, fanlit seminary door, shut tight.

Afternoon light fired a rosy gleam on the few windows which were left. But so many were boarded up. She stood and counted how many panes were gone: ninety of them! Bare sills replaced torn sashes.

A chaise wheeled by on the Scotland Road; its rider peered curiously into the yard.

Bernadette sat down on the front stoop, felt the empty house behind her. She imagined how hollowly her footsteps would echo if she walked through the rooms in there. She was discovering memories didn't die as easily as footsteps.

Restlessly she scuffed through the crisp brown leaves to kneel at the base of the dry fountain. How long ago it had been turned off, its rainbow spray smothered by hate!

Moss grew in the fountain circle; Bernadette ran her hand wonderingly over its velvety surface. She remembered her hand in Miriam's and how their hands had come unclasped as she and Paul fled.

After a while, she wandered to the tamarack tree beside Miriam's ell window. Miriam had been forced to leave this countryside she had found beautiful, this house which had sheltered her, the brave teacher who was the closest white person — save one — Miriam had ever known.

And where was the teacher now? Where would she live, what would she do? What would she remember of Canterbury?

The wind in the tamarack boughs sighed and mingled with Bernadette's recollections of Miss Crandall, of Miriam. The memory of Miriam's voice declaring in the courtroom that it had been marvelous to her, this Canterbury school, except for the want of civilized people. Recalling that voice, Bernadette decided the only thing missing in Canterbury was the best thing there was in the world.

That night, Paul came up to her shyly as she was clearing the table.

"I've got something for you."

Bernadette wiped her hands on her apron, reached for the book he held out.

"It's about Hannibal and the Romans. If you stay here I'll finish teaching you how to swim next summer."

Touched and grateful, Bernadette looked up at Paul, and on impulse stood on tiptoe and kissed his cheek. She liked him so much — nearly as much now as his Cousin Jonathan. Then she looked over to Hester, Hester who was watching, her eyes filling with tears.

"Stay, Bernadette," Hester whispered. "You're daughter to me and sister to Rachel."

"She's not sister to me," Paul declared with gruff meaning, then turned his usual fiery red and fled.

She felt so funny about kissing Paul and so torn by Hester that her knees began to buckle. Wordlessly she simply scooped up Rachel and carried her out to the orchard, sat down under a fruit-laden tree.

All-unknowing, sweet Rachel crawled into her lap, circled her arms around Bernadette's neck, pressed against her comfortingly, then collapsed and sucked her thumb sleepily.

Bernadette buried her face in the silken hair; it smelled of sunshine and flowers. "Rachel," she whispered, "remember me . . ."

Her days in Canterbury had begun with Rachel. They were ending with Rachel, too.

She lifted the baby up, held her close, yearningly.

Far below in the great blue meadow, an evening bird swooped swift and free.